FOCUS ON THE

The

Second Choices
Copyright © 2000
Shirley Brinkerhoff

Cover illustration by Paul Casale

A Focus on the Family book
Published by Bethany House Publishers
A Ministry of Bethany Fellowship International
11400 Hampshire Avenue South
Minneapolis, Minnesota 55438
www.bethanyhouse.com

Printed in the United States of America by
Bethany Press International, Minneapolis, Minnesota 55438

Library of Congress Cataloging-in-Publication Data

CIP data applied for

ISBN 1—56179–880–0

---

00 01 02 03 04 05 06 07 / 15 14 13 12 11 10 9 8 7 6 5 4 3 2 1

To the members of
Heritage Baptist Church, Clarks Summit, Pennsylvania
and Grace Brethren Church, Frederick, Maryland
with love and thanks for being a true family

The NIKKI SHERIDAN SERIES
by Shirley Brinkerhoff

❦ *One* ❦

FOR THE FIRST TIME in over a year Nikki Sheridan was back in Millbrook for an entire weekend.

She'd worried about going back, knowing she might run into her father, whom she wasn't yet ready to see. Or worse, someone from Millbrook High, the school she'd attended through her sophomore year. But so far, none of her fears had come true, and Nikki congratulated herself on how well the weekend was going as she drove toward the dry cleaners.

It was unseasonably hot and humid for early October in Ohio. A stream of sweat trickled down her back, and she hoped the wetness didn't show through the thin, white knit of her crop top. She was due to pick up her mother's dry cleaning, but that would have to wait until she'd had something cold to drink, Nikki decided. Especially since, as she knew from experience, it would take more than one trip to carry all her mother's dry cleaning to the car. Making a quick detour for an ice-cold Coke sounded like the best idea she'd had all day.

Nikki parked in front of the 7-Eleven and went inside. She was so intent on getting her drink that she didn't notice the guy at the refrigerator case until she stopped directly behind him. He grabbed a Mountain Dew from the shelf, and his blond hair and number 10 soccer jersey were instantly, painfully, familiar to Nikki. With the recognition came a flood of memories.

She swallowed hard and took a step backward. *I need to get out of here before he sees me.* But with the same quick, sure movements that had made him one of Millbrook High's favorite soccer stars, T.J. slammed the refrigerator door and whirled around on one foot. He stopped dead when he found himself face to face with Nikki.

His brown eyes met her blue ones and for an age-long second, everything stopped. Then T.J.'s eyes darted to one side, then the other. She could sense him struggling to take control of the situation, to act cool and in charge, and she remembered that way he'd always had of sweeping a room with his gaze, as though waiting for the applause to start. She used to think it was awesome, the way he just assumed everyone thought he was great.

"Hey, there, Nikki Sheridan," he said now. "It's been a long time since I've seen you. But you're looking good." His gaze traveled slowly from her face to her feet and back. "You're looking *great*."

Nikki never knew what made her blurt out what she said next. Maybe T.J.'s arrogance. Maybe remnants of her own anger at him, buried so deep she'd stopped admitting it was there.

"Glad you still think so, T.J. Pregnancy does tend to change a person, after all," she shot back.

She had a second of satisfaction, seeing his composure slip. It made her think of glass, shattering in slow motion. His cocky smile hung in place for an instant; then her words began to register in his suddenly troubled eyes. Wrinkles appeared over his eyebrows and his mouth straightened to a flat line.

Then he jerked his head backward so that the shock of blond hair flew back from his forehead, and the attitude returned. "What's that supposed to mean?"

Nikki looked him straight in the eye. "Take a guess, T. J."

His eyes darted side to side again before his gaze settled somewhere near her chin. He gave an exaggerated shrug and unscrewed the top of his Mountain Dew bottle deliberately. "I'm not into guessing games," he said, then tilted his head back for a long series of gulps. Nikki stared straight at him, as though daring him to meet her eyes. Instead, he pushed past her to the counter, keeping his back turned toward her.

Nikki felt her knees begin to shake; the tips of her fingers started to tingle. She knew she needed to sit down fast, so she turned and pushed her way out the glass doors of the 7-Eleven into the blinding sunlight. She was backing her blue Mazda out of the parking lot before she realized she had completely forgotten the Coke.

Back at the house where she'd grown up, lugging in two slippery armfuls of plastic-sheathed suits and dresses from the Mazda, Nikki tried unsuccessfully to shut the meeting with T.J. out of her mind. Instead, all the things she could have said to him, things she *wished* she had said, kept popping up inside her head.

She hung the last of the suits in her mother's closet, adjusting the neckline of a shell-pink silk jacket which drooped precariously off the side of one hanger, then went down the hall to her bedroom.

She stopped in the doorway and glanced around at the room that was filled with memories of her first 16 years. It was decorated with the best of furniture, chosen on the advice of the expert at Ethan Allen. Each rug and picture complemented the scheme, though they had little to do with Nikki's tastes. She remembered the day of her thirteenth birthday vividly, and how satisfied her mother had been with the results. "It looks like something right out of *Seventeen*, don't you think?" Rachel had said, standing where Nikki now stood, arms crossed over her chest, one toe tapping slightly as she waited for her daughter's affirmation.

But Nikki had felt then as she did now, that it was the room of a stranger. Ruffles had never interested her much, particularly on bedspreads and curtains. *I'll take my room at Gram and Grandpa's over this, any day.* She crossed to the bed and dropped down on it with a sigh, hugging a pillow to her chest and resting her chin on it. No matter how she felt about it, this room was about the only thing in her life that hadn't changed drastically in the last year.

From her seat on the bed, Nikki could see her reflection in the wide, white-framed dresser mirror. She stared at the blue-eyed image and struggled to remember who she had been on the day of that last date with T.J., nearly a year and a half ago. A sudden look of confusion passed over the face of the mirror image. *A year and a half? How could life change so much in just a year and a half?*

Nikki shook her head back and forth slowly at the thought, watching her dark hair brush the shoulders of her white crop top. "You didn't have a clue what you were getting into, did you, kiddo?" she whispered aloud to her reflection. "You couldn't see past T.J.'s soccer jersey, past the blond hair and charm."

She blew a long sigh through pursed lips. "And you *sure* couldn't see what it felt like being pregnant with Evan!" She could still feel the shock and confusion, even terror, of the summer day she'd found out she was pregnant. Meanwhile, T. J. had gone right on being the great Millbrook High jock, as far as she had heard. While she was trying to pick up the shreds of her life in Michigan, T. J. went right on winning soccer awards, graduating with his own friends from his own high school. While Nikki sat huddled on the window seat in the bedroom at her grandparents' house in Michigan, crying from loneliness and scared to death of going through labor, T. J. had been right here hanging out. *Probably partying every weekend, at that!*

Oh, there were a lot of things she wished she had said to T. J. at the 7-Eleven—a *lot* of things. Anger churned inside her, and warning voices went off in her head. She'd had to deal with so much anger since the last time she'd seen T. J.—anger at her parents, anger at herself. And she'd learned to do it, she thought. Learned how to forgive and get past all the anger and get on with her life. But just when she thought she'd finally managed to do it, the past reached out with tentacles like an octopus and dragged her right back. If she could have one wish—just one—it would be to get free of the past once and for all. Free of anger that exploded inside her without warning, as it had in the 7-Eleven today.

But anger at T. J.—that was different, wasn't it? If there ever was someone she had a right to be angry at, it was T. J. She thought back to those first few times they'd gone out. T. J. had acted like he really cared about her, like he wanted to know everything about her— what she thought and who she really was, deep inside. But once he got her to sleep with him, it was all over. He never gave her the time of day after that. Nikki knew that what she'd done was wrong, but still—to just drop her like that! Forgiving would never be an option, not with him.

The warning voices got even louder, but she refused to listen. She pushed herself up off the bed and crossed the room to the mirror where she gathered the dark hair up off her perspiring neck and twisted it into an elastic. She'd be headed back home to Michigan by tomorrow morning. Back to normal life, where she'd never have to worry about seeing T.J. again. With effort, Nikki shelved the thoughts about what had happened in the 7-Eleven, then went to the kitchen to find her mother.

Rachel was unloading the dishwasher. Her hair, permed and dyed the color of winter wheat, hid her face as she bent over to lift the silverware bin to the counter. When she heard Nikki, she turned and smiled.

"Nicole, you're back. Did you get all the dry cleaning put away?"

Nikki nodded and went to the fridge.

"Thirsty?" Rachel asked. "I found some root beer that was left, way in the back, when I was cleaning out the refrigerator this morning."

Nikki reached for a can, then stopped. Root beer had always been her father's favorite. These cans were probably left over from him. She poured a glass of iced tea instead. "Want some of this, Mother?"

Rachel shook her head. "No, thanks. I've been drinking it all afternoon." She glanced at Nikki's face, then turned back to the silverware drawer she was filling. "Are you . . . doing okay, Nikki?"

Nikki sat on the counter, swinging her legs as she drank. "I guess that depends on what you mean by 'okay.' "

Rachel straightened up and looked directly at her. "You look as though something's pretty heavy on your mind."

Nikki drained the last of her tea and gave a short laugh. "Well, that shouldn't be too surprising, should it? Let's see, now. My father leaves to go live with another woman, my mother's left here totally alone—yeah, I guess you could say I have a few things on my mind."

Rachel held up one hand to stop her. "Nikki, don't. I wasn't talking about that. I just got the sense that something else might be bothering you since you got back from the cleaners, but I don't mean to pry." She dropped a spatula into the stoneware pitcher she used as a holder for kitchen utensils, then slid a knife into its slot in the wooden knife block with a little *click.*

"I don't how you can be so calm about all this," Nikki said. "Doesn't it drive you crazy, what Dad's doing?"

Rachel nodded. "If I dwell on it."

"So what are you doing? Just pretending this isn't even happening?" Nikki regretted the words as soon as she said them, but it was too late to take them back.

Rachel turned to her daughter with a stricken look in her eyes. "Is that what you think, Nikki? That I'm just in some kind of denial?"

"Mother, I'm sorry! I didn't mean to hurt you—"

"What hurts me is that you don't seem to understand what I *am* doing—and if you don't, you can't be a part of it." She took a glass out of the dishwasher and put it in the cupboard. "I know exactly what your father's doing—I face the truth of it every day. And I pray over it. All the time. And I leave the door open for God to work, because we don't have any idea what He's going to do here." She lifted out another glass and looked at her daughter over the top of it. "And I hope you'll pray with me, Nikki."

"I'm trying. I just have a lot of mixed feelings about Dad right now. Sometimes I pray really hard for him. And sometimes, I'm furious with him."

Rachel reached over to where Nikki sat on the counter and touched her cheek gently. "And sometimes, I expect it hurts too much to even think about him, let alone pray for him. Am I even close?"

Nikki nodded. "Very close."

Rachel smiled. "I think that's pretty normal. And I'm here any time you need to talk. Just let me tell you in the meantime how much it means to me to have you here, Nikki, even for a weekend. I know it wasn't easy for you to come back. Just know that I appreciate it." She bent to retrieve more utensils from the dishwasher, then straightened up and faced her daughter. "And that I hope you'll come back again, soon."

Nikki looked away, her eyes stinging with quick tears. The phone rang, and she slid off the counter quickly, glad for the diversion. She was even gladder to find it was Jeff. She motioned to her mother that she would take the call on the deck and stepped outside through the sliding glass doors.

"How're you doing?" Jeff asked.

Nikki kicked off her sandals and curled up in the shade of the Norway maple which shadowed one of the thickly-cushioned lounge chairs. She reveled in the knowledge that things between her and Jeff were finally going exactly the way she wanted them to. At times the relationship seemed almost too good to be true.

"Everything's fine." She hesitated, then added, "It's just kind of—weird, you know? Being back here in Millbrook and all."

Jeff murmured a sympathetic "Hmm" on the other end of the line, and waited for her to go on.

"Especially with my mother."

"Oh, yeah?" he asked, sounding surprised. "I would've thought that would be the best part of the whole situation."

Nikki sighed. "It is, in a way. It's just that it's like she's turned into this totally different person."

"Nik, people are *supposed* to change when they get things straight with the Lord."

"Yeah, but overnight? She's like this—*stranger* now. When she went with me to see Evan a couple of weeks ago, she just melted. Right in front of my eyes, she turned into the all-American grandma, you know? After all those months of not even admitting he existed! It was so freaky."

Nikki went on to describe the extra visit her baby's adoptive parents had allowed them to make, even though the open adoption arrangement specified only two visits per year. Evan, at eight months, had been fascinated with Rachel, hardly taking his eyes off her face the entire time they were there. Nikki made it sound as funny as she could in the retelling. But she wasn't ready to tell anyone yet, even Jeff, about how deeply it had touched her to see Rachel holding Evan close, kissing his pudgy graham-cracker-crumbed cheeks and never even noticing the chewed-up bits that dropped all over her immaculate silk top.

"So, are you complaining or what?" Jeff asked when she finished.

"*No!* I'm just—just acclimating, that's all." Nikki ignored his low whistle, and went on before he could tease her about the word. "I'm glad, okay? Very glad. I just feel like I prayed and prayed for her, then I got left in the dust when she changed so fast. Jeff, she hardly ever even bad-mouths my dad anymore!"

"You almost sound like that bothers you," he said.

"Jeff, of course it doesn't bother me! It just takes some getting used to, that's all." There was a click on the phone line. "Jeff, could you hold on for a minute? There's another call coming in and it may be for Mother."

Nikki switched lines and said hello.

"Nikki? Is that you?" Without waiting for an answer, the voice continued. "Listen, this is T.J. We need to talk."

Nikki stared at the phone for a second, then deliberately switched back to Jeff.

❧ *Two* ❧

ON SUNDAY AFTERNOON, Nikki made the four-hour trip back to her grandparents' house in Rosendale, Michigan, her mind still full of the situation with T.J. She was hardly aware of the vast fields of golden cornstalks flying by on either side of the blue Mazda, or of where exactly she was on I–94.

I should never have said that to T.J., she berated herself. *Mentioning the word 'pregnancy' just made him curious—curious enough to call. That was one of the stupidest things I've done all year.* She glanced into the reflection of her blue eyes in the rearview mirror, and made a face. *And I've done plenty of stupid things, that's for sure!*

She had felt a storm of emotions when she found out she was pregnant with Evan, and one of the strongest was embarrassment. To Lauren and the other girls in T.J.'s crowd—Millbrook upperclassmen Nikki had looked up to for as long as she could remember—it was fine to sleep around. Even cool. But getting pregnant—*that* was considered truly stupid.

Nikki signaled a right turn and moved out of the passing lane to let a semi roar by. She was amazed at how easily she'd been taken in by such an upside-down way of looking at things through most of junior high and her sophomore year. Now that she'd had Evan and understood where sleeping with a guy could lead, her ideas were totally different.

I didn't have a clue! she thought. All she'd been able to think of back then was that she couldn't even sleep with a guy and get it "right." One time—*one time!*—and she got pregnant.

Nikki had ended up cutting off all contact with friends in Ohio. Instead of going home to Millbrook after the summer, she stayed on in Michigan with her grandparents. The plan was that no one back in Millbrook would ever find out just how stupid she'd been, and it had worked. Till now, at least. Till she opened her big mouth to T.J. Now the news would probably be all over town in hours.

The exit sign for Kalamazoo slid by on her right, and Nikki realized how far she'd driven without paying close attention to the road. She straightened up in her seat and took a deep breath, determined to be more careful.

It'll just be better for everyone if I don't go back to Ohio again, she told herself. It would be hard on her mother, who finally, *finally*, seemed to want the relationship Nikki had longed for all these years.

"Can you come back next week?" Rachel had asked when they said goodbye in the driveway. "Or at least the week after that?"

At first Nikki had planned to say yes. Something new and wonderful had been born in her heart when she watched Rachel reach out in love to tiny Evan. Nikki had known then that, for the first time she could remember, she *wanted* to spend time with Rachel.

But I can't do that now, not after what happened this weekend. I need to stay as far away from Millbrook as I can.

Nikki switched the radio on, trying to turn her thoughts in another direction. She took the exit for 131 and headed north toward Grand Rapids, but her thoughts circled right back to where they'd started.

Sometimes it seemed there was no end to the fallout from that one night she'd slept with T.J. Now there was eight-month-old Evan—settled with the Shiveleys, his adoptive parents, but never far from Nikki's mind and heart.

And then there was the situation with her own parents. Logically, Nikki knew she wasn't the cause of their breakup. And her grandparents kept reinforcing that. "Your getting pregnant didn't force your father to make this decision," Gram had said over and over in response to Nikki's feelings of guilt. "People are responsible for their own choices. Your father is responsible for what he chooses, no matter what you did that embarrassed or shamed him."

Still, Nikki couldn't help thinking, *if I hadn't gotten pregnant, hadn't gone ahead and had the baby, hadn't—*

"That's enough!" she stopped herself. "I'm not responsible for what Dad's doing, I'm *not*. All I can do now is be there for Mom as often as I can." *And pray a lot, for both of them,* she added to herself.

Nikki's eyelids grew heavy and she rolled down the window beside her. She could feel how much cooler the air had turned as she traveled north and west toward Lake Michigan. Far away, to her left, a line of low hills was beginning to show, hills that signaled she was getting closer to Rosendale and the lakeshore.

She took a long drink from her can of Coke and resolved to pay more attention to the changing leaves and the wide, blue sky instead of getting stuck inside her thoughts. But it didn't work.

Now, on top of everything else, because she'd shot off her mouth at the wrong time, T.J. might find out about Evan—about what had really happened from those few minutes of intimacy. Nikki was taken back by the anger she felt, just from being forced to remember.

She'd been so sure she'd finally worked through *all* her anger, so glad to get rid of the weight of it. The anger at her parents had been the hardest to get rid of, because at the time when Nikki had needed them most, David and Rachel Sheridan hadn't been there for her. It had taken months and months to work through all her feelings over that, but she finally had. She'd been angry at herself, too, and even at God for a while.

Great! Just when I thought I was finished with all that, I have to run into T.J.! She gripped the steering wheel till her fingers ached. There was more anger inside her than she'd ever imagined. Undealt with. Unresolved.

Keep your mind on the road, Nikki, she told herself, trying to divert her thoughts. *On the road, and on the fact that you're almost home, and on the homework you have to do there, and . . .*

It was nearly an hour later, just a few miles from home, that Nikki found herself struggling again with sleepiness. Her eyelids were drooping but she didn't want to stop, not this close to home. She exited off the highway and braked at the stop sign, ready to start her turn onto the quiet side road to Rosendale.

But as she did, a late-model gold Cirrus roared past on her right at high speed, barreling through the stop sign without even slowing. Nikki jerked awake, holding her breath as the Cirrus missed an oncoming Subaru by inches. The green Subaru screeched to a stop and a dark-haired, fortyish man jumped out, yelling in the direction of the rapidly shrinking gold car, shaking both fists above his head in fury. At last the man shook his head in the direction the Cirrus had disappeared, got back into his car, and drove off. Nikki still sat at the stop sign, trembling all over, her heart pounding so fast she thought her chest would explode.

She had recognized the Cirrus immediately as Chad Davies'. She'd dated Chad the winter before, when he'd first moved to town. His family was so messed up it almost made Nikki feel better by comparison. Chad's drinking and anger and erratic behavior had finally made her break off their relationship, but she'd never been able to quit worrying about him.

That was crazy! she thought, replaying the near-accident in her mind. *Like he never even saw the stop sign.* She couldn't help wondering if Chad was drinking again. He'd talked about getting help with his drinking the spring before, and word was out that he'd quit over the summer. But after what she'd just seen . . . Nikki shook her head, then checked with extra care before she pulled onto the Rosendale road.

Nikki was still trying to sort out her confusion about Chad when she got home to her grandparents'. Their blue clapboard house, set at the edge of a steep bluff, nestled against the side of the heavily forested dune in one direction and looked out over Lake Michigan in the other. Just the sight of the quiet street that dead-ended at their front yard seemed to help Nikki breathe more slowly, to relax her white-knuckled grip on the steering wheel.

I've got to put Chad out of my mind for now, she thought. She knew how her grandparents felt about him after last year. It wasn't just that he'd driven under the influence and ended up hitting Gallie, their beloved Golden Retriever, and breaking the dog's leg. That was bad enough, but Chad's lack of reaction had been far worse. He'd made no apologies, given no explanations other than to blame the icy road, and had seemed to act cockier than ever. The last thing she wanted was for his name to come up in the conversation this evening.

Nikki took a deep breath and looked around, depending as always on the beauty to calm her. With summer vacationers gone, Rosendale took on a different character somehow, as though the entire village breathed a collective sigh of relief with the coming of autumn. The tourists had finally gone home, and the beach and pier and myriad boardwalk paths over the dunes belonged to the townspeople again.

She pulled into the driveway and put the Mazda into park. Lake Michigan spread as far as she could see behind the blue clapboard house. For 18 years she'd spent every summer here with her grandparents, and she'd grown used to humid days when lake and sky merged at the horizon in a milky, indistinct whiteness. But in the last year, since she'd come to live here permanently, Nikki had grown to love the clarity that autumn brought to the air. With the humidity gone, she could see miles out onto the lake, all the way to where the water met the sky in a dark blue line straight as a ruler.

She smiled at the memory of herself as an eight-year-old, the day Grandpa told her Chicago was on the other side of the water. She could remember squinting till her cheeks ached, convinced she could see the city if she just tried hard enough.

Less welcome was the sight of the Allens' summer house next door, quiet and deserted now. Jeff was all the way across the state in Ann Arbor, at the University of Michigan. Dr. and Mrs. Allen were back in Chicago with the twins. And Carly—Nikki shook her head at the thought that still seemed so hard to believe—Carly was at an eating disorders clinic, battling bulimarexia.

The hot cinnamon scent of Gram's peach pie reached Nikki through the open kitchen window, and brought her back to the present. "Hey!" she called, running up the concrete steps to the kitchen door, "I'm back!"

The touch of Indian summer in the air made it pleasant to sit on the screened porch after they finished dinner, enjoying still-warm peach pie topped with scoops of cold vanilla ice cream. Gram and Grandpa sat in the white wicker rockers, and Gallie lay docilely between them, but Nikki knew his sleepy look was just a guise. At the mere suggestion of a falling crumb, the Golden Retriever would be on his feet in an instant. Every few seconds one brown eye opened lazily, just to check.

Nikki settled herself among the porch swing cushions, noting how early darkness blanketed the lake these days. Only a low line of lights from a barge far offshore showed on the water. But lights from other porches, other kitchen windows, now winked on up and down the shore.

Grandpa stretched his long legs out in front of him, closed his eyes for a minute, and sighed. "This is great. Wish I could sit out here all evening."

"Are you still working on that article about plankton?" Nikki asked. As a retired biology professor, Roger Nobles now was in some demand as a writer for nature and wildlife journals.

He opened his eyes and grinned. "Oh, yeah. Trouble is, it was due last week—so that's just about all I'm doing these days, around the clock." He reached across to rub his wife's back lovingly. "That was another great pie, Carole."

"And the last one of the year, for sure. At least the last one made from fresh peaches," Gram answered. She set her empty plate on the wicker end table, ignoring Gallie's hopeful look, and rested her head against the back of the rocker. "Seems nice to have just the three of us here for a change, doesn't it? Nikki, tell us about your trip before you get to all that homework you said you have waiting."

Nikki sorted through all that had happened as she savored the last mouthful of warm, sweet peach slices. The part about Chad running the stop sign she would leave out. And T.J.—she would definitely skip that part, too.

"Mother's doing really good, I think," she began. "In fact, sometimes it's hard to believe she's the same person. She's meeting with people at her church in this thing she calls an accountability group or a prayer group—something like that. They pray and have a Bible study and stuff. I think it's really helping her handle what's going on with Dad."

There was enough light from the kitchen doorway for Nikki to see Gram and Grandpa glance at each other, then join hands across the wicker end table. "There were times in the last 30 years—lots of them—when we felt like giving up praying for her," Gram said to Nikki. "But I'm sure glad now that we didn't."

Nikki shook her head. "It must run in the genes or something. Now she's praying for Dad that same way." She put her plate on the swing beside her, the crumpled napkin on top of it. "I don't think this is the same kind of situation, though, you know?"

"Why's that, Nikki?" Grandpa asked.

Nikki shrugged. "Well, it doesn't exactly look promising, if you know what I mean. My Dad's already moved in with this other woman, and he's trying to act like he's a father to her kids." She swallowed hard at the stab of pain that thought caused her. "So I don't see much chance of him changing his mind now."

" 'Faith has nothing to do with the probability or the improbability of a circumstance,' " Grandpa said, his voice quiet.

"What'd you just say?" Nikki asked.

Grandpa repeated himself, then added, "It's a quote that helped keep me praying about Rachel all those years," he answered. "It's from George Mueller."

"Who was George Mueller?"

"He lived in England in the 1800s. He decided he wanted to show everybody that God answers prayer, so he took in many hundreds of orphans and supported them totally by praying for them. The answers to prayer he got were amazing. Sometimes, when I felt like giving up on Rachel, I'd read Mueller's journal."

Nikki considered his words for a moment and thought how much she wanted answers to some of her prayers. She was about to ask for more details on Mueller when the phone rang. "I'll get it," she said. She gathered up the pie plates on her way to the kitchen and got to the phone on the fourth ring, just before the answering machine took it.

"Nikki?" The voice was brisk and businesslike, and she could picture Hollis on the other end of the line, toying with the ends of her short, straight brown hair as she always did. She wondered how Hollis always managed to sound so exactly like what she was—the editor of the Howellsville High School paper, chasing a story. "Remember how, after you spoke about abortion at that tea a few weeks ago, Noel and I said we wanted to talk to you?"

Gram's best friend, Arleta, had organized an outreach tea for women and teen girls in early September. Nikki and two local women had been asked to give short testimonies before the special speaker, telling how God had changed their lives. Nikki had refused at first, but Arleta had prodded her through both her reluctance and fear. And it was at that tea that Nikki's mother had finally quit running from God.

"I didn't really say all that much about abortion at the tea. I was just explaining what happened to me," Nikki told Hollis now, picking her words carefully. "Actually, I was hoping you'd be more interested in some of the other stuff I brought up, about God and all."

"Right," Hollis said, her tone dismissive. "I'm sure we'll get around to that, too. Someday. Could you eat lunch with Noel and me tomorrow? We could talk then."

Nikki hesitated for just a second before she answered. She could never avoid feeling uneasy around Hollis, who always seemed so totally self-confident and in control. "Sure, I guess I can do that," she said at last.

They agreed to meet at Burger King the next day, and Nikki immediately started planning how she could talk Keesha into coming along for moral support.

Because Nikki and Keesha had been the only two visibly pregnant students at Howellsville High School the year before, a friendship had developed between them. So far Nikki hadn't really been able to make other close friends there. She'd been too self-concious about her all-too-obvious pregnancy, too wrapped up in the other crises going on in her life. Now, though, she was ready—even longing—to make some new friends. Hollis and Noel, however, were the last people she would have chosen.

Gram's figure appeared in the kitchen doorway. "Everything okay, honey?" she asked, studying Nikki's face.

Nikki sighed. "Yeah. Just—some stuff going on at school I didn't plan on." She glanced at the kitchen clock. "I better go upstairs and get my homework done. And I need to make some calls. But I don't want to leave you with all this mess—"

Gram waved a hand in the air. "Stop coddling me! It's been over a year since the stroke, and I can certainly handle a few dishes." She grinned and hugged her granddaughter. "It's a good excuse to get your grandfather in here to help, anyway. We do some of our best talking when he's got a Brillo pad in his hand."

Nikki made her way upstairs and surveyed the stack of books and notebooks on her dresser with dismay. *It'll take hours to finish all this*, she thought. She picked up her Spanish book from the top of the pile, then set it back down. It was almost impossible to keep thoughts of T.J. from flooding her mind again the minute she was alone.

Maybe I'll just call Jeff and say hello before I start, she thought, longing to hear his voice. She took a step toward the hall phone table, then stopped. She knew that talking to Jeff could put her even further behind, because they never seemed to talk less than an hour these days. On the other hand, when she was talking to him, all the problems took a backseat. She stood halfway between the books and the bedroom door, undecided.

I'll keep it short, she promised herself at last, and went to get the phone.

❧ *Three* ❧

ON MONDAY MORNING Nikki armed herself with words Jeff had said the night before.

"Why are you so nervous about this, Nik?" Jeff had asked when she told him about Hollis's invitation to lunch.

"You don't know Hollis and Noel! I'm afraid they just want to argue the whole abortion issue. Then they'll probably write an editorial about how ignorant pro-lifers are for the school paper!" she'd told him. "I'm no good at debating, you know that. I'd rather tell them about God and what He's done in my life."

"Don't let 'em intimidate you, Nik," Jeff told her. "If you're scared, you'll get defensive, and you don't want to come across that way. If I were you, I wouldn't try to win with medical facts or anything. I'd just tell them what you know, after having to make that decision yourself, I mean."

Tell them what I know. Just tell them what I know. The words kept playing in her mind as she drove toward the high school. She hadn't been able to get through on Keesha's line, so her first goal for the morning was to corner Keesha at their side-by-side lockers and talk her into coming to Burger King as a backup.

She was so intent on her own plans that the commotion in the school parking lot didn't register at first. All she knew was that the driveway to the parking lot was blocked when she tried to turn in off the street.

She drummed her fingers against the black steering wheel impatiently, craning her neck to find out the cause of the holdup. Students milled about on the sidewalks, standing in groups or sitting on the grass. But no one was actually moving toward the doors of the school. The cars ahead of Nikki rolled perhaps five feet in slow motion, then stopped, rolled ahead again, and stopped. At this rate, she'd never catch Keesha at the locker.

Nikki rolled her window down and stuck her head out. From this new vantage point, she could see two police cars parked near the entrance of the parking lot, and a Channel 16 panel truck parked behind them, its rear end protruding into the driveway, causing the turtle-like crawl that she and the cars ahead of her were doing. Eventually even that stopped.

"Hey! What's going on?" she asked two guys whom she recognized vaguely as freshmen. They stood on the sidewalk watching, thumbs hooked under the shoulder straps of their backpacks.

"Just look at the school and you'll see," one of them answered. He jerked his head in the direction of the building and Nikki's eyes opened wide as she took in what he was pointing at. Words in black spray paint were scrawled across the front of the school, so large she could make them out from where she sat, and Nikki cringed as she read them. Many of the words cursed teachers and administration, as well as specific students. In between the curses were "Kill Mendoza" and "Nuke Peabody." Mr. Peabody was the principal, and Ms. Mendoza was Nikki's Current Events teacher and advisor for the school paper.

For a minute Nikki sat speechless, staring in horror at the angry, dark scrawls. A chill ran down her spine. She wrapped her arms around herself, as though to ward off the sudden cold.

She turned again to the freshmen. "Okay, I can see it's a mess out here. But why won't they let us inside the building? Did that get vandalized, too?"

The boy shrugged. "We don't know. Somebody just said the

police are checking everything out before they'll let us anywhere near the building."

The other freshman added, "It's in case somebody put bombs inside or something, I think."

"You're *kidding* . . ." Nikki began, but both boys looked at her as if to say they'd expected a lot more intelligence from a senior, and she said no more out loud. Inside, though, her mind was racing. *This is* Howellsville, *not some place where people go nuts and start putting bombs in the school!*

Nikki eventually gave up waiting and parked the Mazda along the side of the driveway, then stood around in the parking lot like everyone else seemed to be doing. She finally picked Keesha out of a group of students clustered around the Howellsville High School sign and headed toward her. Keesha was easy to spot, with her bright orange top and gold hoop earrings that hung halfway to her shoulders. *She must be in the middle of telling a story*, Nikki thought, seeing the gold hoops sway wildly as Keesha gestured with arms and hands. The students around her were laughing the way people always did when Keesha got going.

"Hey, Keesha," Nikki said when she finally reached her friend's side.

"Nik! You're missing all the excitement! Where've you been?"

"In line, like everybody else," Nikki said, "waiting for half an hour just to get into the parking lot."

"It's crazy, isn't it?" Keesha nodded toward the spray-painted building and rolled her eyes. "Somebody sure had a lot to get off their chest, didn't they?"

The other students in the group chimed in with comments. Everybody had suggestions as to who did the spray painting, and why, it seemed. Nikki listened in amazement to some of the names brought up as possible suspects. After half an hour or so the talk began to die down.

"Listen, Keesha, could I talk to you for a minute?" Nikki asked, her voice quiet. Keesha nodded, and they moved a few steps away from the group.

"What's up?" Keesha asked. She swung her backpack off her

shoulder and onto the grass, then ran both hands through her inch-long hair as she spoke.

"I need you to come to Burger King with me at lunch. Remember that tea Arleta had in September? And I told you Hollis and Noel said they wanted to talk to me about what I said there?"

Keesha's hands stopped, halfway through her hair, and she narrowed her eyes at Nikki. "Hollis and Noel? I'd stay away from those two, if I was you."

Nikki gave an exasperated sigh. "All they want to do is *talk*, okay? It's just that—well—they mostly seem to want to talk about abortion."

Keesha's glance darted back toward the other students, and she took a step away. "Why? And what's this got to do with me?"

"I have no idea why! Probably because they always like to prove they're right. But I thought you could come along and—and—you know, tell them how you—"

"Nik, keep your voice down, would you? You *know* there's no way I'm gonna tell people that I . . ."

"Okay, then," Nikki broke in. "You don't have to. I just want you to be there. Help me give them some reasons why abortion isn't right. And so I won't be so nervous, you know? You could be like a—a one-person support group."

"But Nik, if I come, they'll wonder why. They asked you, not me." She smirked. "Besides, those two are way too high and mighty to want me along."

"Keesha, *please*. We're just going to Burger King. It's not like you need a special invitation."

Keesha looked around uneasily. "I don't know if I should. I'll think about it and tell you later."

Nikki had to be satisfied with that, because the principal appeared at the front entrance then with a bullhorn in his hand. While Howellsville students seldom paid much attention to Mr. Peabody, even his voice commanded attention when it was amplified to this level. "THANK YOU FOR YOUR PATIENCE, STUDENTS. THE BUILDING'S BEEN CLEARED FOR US TO ENTER, SO CLASSES WILL RESUME ON THE NORMAL SCHEDULE. GO TO THE

ROOM WHERE YOU WOULD NORMALLY HAVE YOUR SEC-
OND PERIOD CLASS.

"LET'S KEEP THIS AS ORDERLY AS WE CAN AND NOT
WASTE ANY MORE CLASS TIME. SENIORS, IF YOU'LL ENTER
THE BUILDING FIRST, PLEASE. THEN JUNIORS, THEN SOPH-
OMORES. NOW LET'S GET GOING AND SEE IF WE CAN MAKE
THIS THE BEST MONDAY YET. THERE'LL BE ANNOUNCE-
MENTS ONCE EVERYONE'S IN CLASS AND SETTLED."

Bored with standing in the parking lot for over an hour, most
students turned and started to file inside at Mr. Peabody's request.
Nikki and Keesha were separated as soon as they reached the doors,
and Nikki headed for her Current Events class. She'd just settled
into her seat and was searching through her backpack when Chad
dropped into the seat beside her. She was already edgy, knowing
she hadn't finished all the reading Ms. Mendoza had assigned on
capital punishment because the phone call with Jeff had gone on far
longer than she'd planned. Facing Chad this early in the morning
did nothing to improve her mood.

"Hey, Babe," he said with a smirk, "how's it going?"

"It's going just fine, Chad," she answered. "And my name is not
'*Babe.*'"

Chad snapped his fingers as though surprised. "Now how could
I forget that, I wonder?"

Nikki looked up at him with annoyance and wondered what it
was she'd ever found attractive about him last year. The combina-
tion of blond hair and coffee-black eyes and eyebrows was as startling as ever, but he no longer made her heart beat faster each time
he walked into the room. Still, they'd been friends as well as dated,
and had spent hours and hours talking about the problems their
families were going through.

Nikki couldn't help but worry about how he'd been driving the
day before. She was just about to bring up the subject when he
pushed the nearly-white blond hair back from his forehead and
waggled his dark eyebrows at her suggestively. "So, *Nicole*, you
want to get together again sometime soon?"

Nikki's irritation erupted. "Chad, would you just knock it *off*?"

She sighed and went back to searching out her homework.

He leaned both elbows on her desk and stared at her. "Nikki! I'm serious and you don't even know it, do you? I need to talk to you." His sudden change of tone caught her off guard. She turned and stared back, so close she could see the yellow flecks in his dark eyes. She thought, not for the first time, how impossible it was to read those eyes.

"Chad, do you happen to remember that I'm going out with another guy? Jeff Allen?"

"Oh, yeah," he said, one side of his mouth twisting upward. "You don't have to remind me about *Jeff*. I met him once, remember? Don't tell me—he's the preacher, right?"

"What are you talking about?" she asked, annoyed. "He's a freshman at U of M—"

"He's what they used to call a 'goody two-shoes,' that's what he is." Chad snickered. "I bet that's an experience for you, Nik, going out with a preacher type! Bet you two have some really hot times!"

Furious, Nikki started to defend Jeff, but Ms. Mendoza held up a hand for quiet.

"Chad! Nikki! I'm sure you're having a fascinating discussion back there, but with your permission we'd like to get a few important things done here." Nikki's face burned at being singled out, and she slid down a few inches in her seat. Ms. Mendoza went on. "We'll get to the discussion that was scheduled for today eventually, but some of you may need to talk about what happened this morning first—the vandalism, I mean. This is about the most 'current event' we have just now. So let's clear the air." She sat on the front edge of her desk and nodded toward the class, as though to encourage them to speak.

"It doesn't take many brains to figure out what's going on," said Jordan Wright from his seat by the windows. There was a collective groan from several of the students behind Nikki. Jordan could always be counted on for a pronouncement on every situation.

"Really," said Ms. Mendoza, one eyebrow slightly raised. "Then perhaps you'd better put the rest of us in the picture, because I, for one, haven't quite figured it all out yet."

"We have to outlaw weapons. It's that simple."

"Wait a minute. You're making quite a leap here—"

But Jordan wasn't about to miss the chance to state his opinion. "I'm *saying* that there were all kinds of threats painted on the walls out there, right?" He didn't bother to wait for a reply. "Even threats to kill people. So think about all the school shootings in the past couple years. How have most of the people been killed? Guns, right? So you take away the guns, you take away the potential for damage. Get my point?"

"Why don't you try to get a little more *simplistic*, Jordan?" Andrea asked, her words laced with disgust.

"Why doesn't he just try to get a *brain?*" another voice called from the back of the room.

"*Cut!*" Ms. Mendoza broke in. "You all know the ground rules in my classes by now. You're free to give your opinion, but I *won't* allow personal comments that demean other people. So stay on target here. I've asked you to discuss a specific problem, not take potshots at one another."

Several people talked at once, voicing everything from suggestions that the culprits pay for the damage to recommendations that they be forced to serve time doing community service.

Nikki watched Hollis and Noel, surprised at their uncharacteristic silence. They were both writing busily, though, and Nikki thought they must be taking notes for another editorial. Meanwhile, Jerry Simoncelli said that whoever did it ought to have planted bombs so school would be closed for the whole week, maybe even the month—but everyone was used to ignoring him.

Molly Whalin, usually silent in any situation involving more than two people, surprised everyone by speaking up then. "I think we have to see that whoever did this is, like, looking for attention. You know what I mean? Like, they're trying to get someone to help them before they—"

"Oh, cut the garbage, would you?" Chad hissed under his breath. "All you're doing is parroting what you heard in psych class." He was turned halfway around in his chair, so that only Nikki could hear him clearly. She was shocked by the fury in his voice, which seemed out of keeping not only with the class discussion, but also with the Chad she was used to, always so determined to be cool about everything.

Nikki watched Chad's cheeks turn darker and darker red as he listened to the dicussion. Finally it seemed he could hold the words in no longer. "Maybe we should quit playing amateur psychiatrist here and just *ask* the people who did it. They're the only ones who know why they did it."

"Chad, please. I've asked you before not to interrupt," Ms. Mendoza ordered.

"Come off it!" he shot back. "What good can it *possibly* do to sit here pretending to discuss somebody's motives when you don't have the faintest clue?" He turned to face the front of the room and spread his hands wide to emphasize his point. "There could be a *hundred* motives for spray painting stuff like that all over the school—maybe a *thousand*, for all you know. But until you ask whoever did it, you're just playing stupid mind games!"

Ms. Mendoza sighed and asked if anyone else had anything to say, but there was no response. For a moment, Nikki almost felt sorry for her. Chad could be more articulate than most of the teachers in the school when he wanted to, she thought, and it was obvious that he had effectively shut down this discussion.

"All right, then, get out your homework and we'll get to work," Ms. Mendoza said at last.

Nikki looked down at the papers on her desk, unable to shake the feeling that Chad's outburst was about far more than just anger.

With the thought of lunch with Hollis and Noel looming before her, Nikki had worried about paying attention in her classes that morning. She soon realized, however, that no one else was paying attention, either. Nearly everyone was talking about the vandalism. But while they discussed the spray-painted words, Nikki's mind was on what she could possibly say at Burger King. She had seen Hollis and Noel make total fools out of students who disagreed with them in Current Events. And they did it in such a calm, intellectual way—"We're just stating the facts," they always said—that it was impossible to fight back.

Hollis can fire questions at you like bullets, Nikki thought, doodling Jeff's name, intertwined with vines and flowers, in the margin of her Spanish homework. *And I've never been very good at thinking up fast answers.* Normally she thought of all the clever things she *should* have said about 24 hours after the fact. Hollis certainly never had that problem.

By the time she reached the parking lot at lunch time, Nikki was questioning her own sanity. *Why on earth didn't I just say no to Hollis?* She stood beside the blue Mazda for a few moments, searching for a glimpse of Keesha coming her way, trying to remember why she'd agreed to this.

I had the idea You were doing something here, Lord, she prayed silently, scanning the parking lot. *Remember how Mother acted when I spoke? How she came back to You? I guess I thought You might actually use me to help Hollis and Noel know You, too, but now . . .* She shook her head, thinking how unlikely that seemed.

"Come on, Keesha!" she said, under her breath. "I really need you with me right now."

At last Nikki gave up and slid into the driver's seat, wondering how she'd get through this lunch alone. She knew what she believed about abortion, all right. That wasn't the problem. She'd struggled through it all when she was pregnant with Evan, when abortion had looked—at first—like the easiest, most logical way out of an unbelievably tough situation.

She just didn't want to face Hollis and Noel alone. It wasn't until she put the car in reverse and started backing out of the parking space that she heard a quick rap on the passenger side window.

Keesha pulled open the door and slid in easily beside her, wearing a half-apologetic grin. But her words did nothing to soothe Nikki's fears. "Can you just explain why in the world you agreed to go to lunch with these two? Their mouths are practically lethal weapons, girl!"

❧ Four ❧

LUNCH ENDED UP BEING a hurried affair. They'd chosen Burger King because hardly anyone went there anymore and they thought it would be nearly empty. Instead, they got stuck in line behind a succession of wiggly preschoolers and irate young mothers. They ordered more kids' meals than Nikki could count. Several children tore open their free toy right there in line, decided they already had that one, and cried to exchange it.

By the time the girls got their food, Hollis was looking around with distaste.

"I don't think this is quite Hollis's style," Keesha whispered as she and Nikki pushed their paper cups against the silver prongs of the drink dispenser and watched soda foam down in a steady stream.

Nikki elbowed her quickly, hissing "Shhh!" as Noel carried her tray around the corner toward them.

At the table Hollis immediately took charge. "Okay, Nikki," she said, unfolding the paper from around her fish sandwich, "we don't have much time left here."

Nikki made a stab at looking in control herself. "You're right, we don't. So what did you want to talk about?"

"*You* said, back at that tea thing in September, that when you found out you were pregnant, you just assumed you should get an abortion, right?" Hollis asked.

Nikki nodded, chewing.

"So what stopped you?"

Under Hollis's scrutiny, Nikki swallowed her mouthful too fast and choked on the lumpy edges of broiled burger that were scraping their way down her throat. She grabbed for her soda and gulped. Hollis waited wordlessly, pulling at the short brown hair over her temple as she watched.

Sitting calmly beside Hollis, Noel alternately picked at her salad and sipped black coffee. Nikki, her eyes red and watery from choking, couldn't help making a mental note to order black coffee next time. It was far more sophisticated than choking on soda and a Whopper, that was for sure.

"What stopped me?" Nikki said at last, when she could talk again. "Well. That's kind of a long story, of course." She gave a short laugh, wondering how to start.

God was what—or Who, rather—had stopped her. She knew that now. It just wasn't the kind of thing she could say to Hollis or Noel.. And she didn't know how else to explain it.

"I grew up thinking that abortion was just one of many options," she began finally. "I bet almost everybody our age thinks so because it's legal," she added, "but when I started to look into it—really *think* about it—it looked totally different."

Noel pulled her glossy black hair back from her face with both hands, twisted it into a knot at the nape of her neck and looked bored. "Nikki, what we want to know is *why*. *Why* didn't you just have the abortion?" She drummed her fingers against the table top and looked as though she held out little hope for an intelligent answer.

"Well, at first, things just kept getting in the way."

Even Keesha looked at her quizzically, and Nikki remembered that they hadn't even known each other back then.

"Like, when I went to the abortion clinic, there were demonstrators there, and a camera truck from WJRB," Nikki explained. "I didn't want my picture on the news, so I left, thinking I could just go back another time. Then my grandmother had a stroke, and for days we all sat around in the hospital room, wondering whether she'd make it or not. So I couldn't go back to the clinic while all that was going on."

And then there were the pamphlets from the demonstrators that made me actually think about what I was doing, she thought. *And my mother was using my car so I couldn't even drive myself to the clinic even if I did have the time. And then I saw that display in the museum in Grand Rapids*—She shuddered, thinking how the sight of all those tiny fetuses in jars, at different stages of development, had gripped her—even given her chills. That had been the first time she'd ever seen what the life inside her looked like—the life she had been dead set on ending.

It was Keesha's turn to elbow her now, and Nikki looked at her in surprise. Keesha nodded her head toward Hollis, who was speaking.

"I *asked* you, 'What changed your mind?'"

"Oh, sorry. I started remembering, and—well, anyway, I guess it was a lot of different things that all came together at the right time. I had an ultrasound and saw the baby moving around inside of me—" Nikki broke off, unable to speak for a moment because the memory still produced a catch in her throat. The emotion of seeing Evan for the first time, there on the ultrasound screen, was far too personal to share with just anyone.

At her side, Keesha nodded her head in agreement. "It's true. Once you see that baby moving inside you, everything changes. Not that I ever thought about abortion or anything," she added hastily.

Nikki glanced sideways at her in surprise, then remembered how important it was not to give away Keesha's secret. She went on with her own account. "But I think I *knew* I couldn't have an abortion, even before the ultrasound. Because of Gram's stroke."

Noel set her coffee on the table. "I'm not making the connection here."

"People kept telling me, 'This fetus isn't really a human life yet. It can't take care of itself. It can't live without help, it can't make it on its own.' That kind of made sense to me at first. But then I sat by my grandmother's bedside. For about a week she was in a coma from the stroke, and she couldn't do a single thing for herself. There was no way she could have lived on her own. But I *knew* Gram, and I loved her. She was a person whether she could do all that or not. All of a sudden, that argument just didn't hold water for me anymore."

Hollis eyed Nikki even more intently, looking interested in spite of herself. Nikki took a quick sip of soda, then went on. "I wouldn't be honest, though, if I didn't tell you the rest of what was going on. See, I believe God was using all this to make me turn to Him. I knew about God—I'd gone to church a lot with my grandparents and all—but I didn't really know Him personally. And sometimes, when you get into a really tough place in your life, you can hear God better. That was the way it was with me."

There was silence when she finished, silence louder than the noise of the customers all around them. Finally Hollis said, "That's really heavy."

Nikki asked, "Why is it so important to you to talk to me about all this, anyway? I mean, you can read all the pro-life arguments on the Internet or in books ... "

Noel rolled her eyes and jerked her head toward Hollis. "This whole thing was totally her idea."

A look of hurt flashed across Hollis's face before she could hide it, and Nikki suspected suddenly that the relationship between Hollis and Noel was not as perfect as it seemed to be.

"Is it such a crime to want to discuss a subject? To want to find out what other people think?" Hollis demanded. "There're how many millions of abortions in this country every year? I think it'd be pretty stupid *not* to want to discuss it." Her words were a challenge thrown into Noel's face, but Noel sipped her coffee impassively. Nikki found herself wondering if Hollis's words really had that little effect, or if Noel was simply a terrific actor.

There was an uncomfortable silence before Noel spoke again. "Anyway, abortion is one of the issues that's coming up for discussion in Current Events." She gathered up her napkin and cup and stuffed them into the Burger King bag, then looked up and gave a short laugh. "So at least we know a little bit about how the other side thinks now."

Nikki finished her Whopper in disappointment. *They didn't really want to know what I thought, or about God or anything. They just wanted to make sure they'd be ready for a hot debate in class.*

Can you *believe* them?" Keesha asked, rolling her eyes as she looked at Nikki across the seat of the blue Mazda. "They don't have a clue what it's like to be pregnant, do they? Not a *clue!*"

"I guess not," Nikki said, craning her neck to see if the lane was clear. She pulled out of the Burger King parking lot and headed for the high school. "But the real issue is that all they wanted was to make sure we disagreed. So now they know where I stand so they can shoot me down in the Current Events discussion! I mean, it was bad enough when I thought they just wanted to argue this thing privately, but in *class?*"

"I don't know if you got the whole picture, Nik." Keesha rummaged through her bag and pulled out her lipstick. She started re-doing her lips, leaning forward to peer into the mirror on the backside of the visor. "I mean, I think that's what Noel seemed to want. But I had the feeling that Hollis was really interested in some of what you said."

Nikki pumped the brakes to a gentle stop as the light ahead turned yellow. "You know, Keesha, now that I think about it, we've never actually talked about God, you and me. I don't really know where you stand on the whole issue."

Keesha froze, lipstick in mid-air, then swung around to look at Nikki. "Well, you know I'm a Christian!"

Nikki shook her head. "No, I don't, not really. You've never said a word about it."

Keesha looked annoyed as she resumed her makeup repairs. "You know my mother's been dragging me to church since the day I was born, practically."

"Yeah, but Keesha, *that* doesn't make you a Christian! Grandpa always says that going to church doesn't make you a Christian any more than going to a barn makes you a horse."

Keesha burst out laughing. "That sounds like your grandfather! Anyway, you can relax, because my mother's basically been telling me the same thing all my life. I know you have to believe that Jesus died for your sins and ask for forgiveness and for Him to come into your heart."

"So, did you?"

"Well, of course. My mother told me what to say and I repeated it, back when I was five or six or something." Keesha snapped the top back on her lipstick and dropped it into her bag. "Feel better now?"

Nikki didn't reply for a minute. "I don't know," she said at last. "Isn't becoming a Christian supposed to be something that matters *right now* in your life? I mean, it's got to be more than something that happened 10 years ago and you never thought about again."

"Who says I never thought about it again?" Keesha asked indignantly.

Nikki glanced sideways at her. "Oh, Keesha, I'm sorry! I didn't mean to be rude. I was just kind of—thinking out loud, I guess. Trying to figure it out." They pulled into a parking space in the school lot and Nikki turned off the ignition. "I mean, you've never said a word to me about being a Christian before."

"Well, so what?" Keesha demanded. "Neither have you!"

"Of course I have!" Nikki said. "When Jeff and I took you to the hospital to have Serena, we prayed with you, remember? And—and when I was getting ready to give my testimony at Arleta's tea, I know I talked to you about it then."

Keesha looked her straight in the eye. "No, you didn't. I mean, yes, you and Jeff prayed with me, and yes, you *complained* a lot about having to talk at Arleta's tea. But you never actually talked about whether or not *I* was a Christian. I always wondered if you were ever gonna get around to it."

Nikki looked at her, speechless.

"You always say we're friends, Nikki," Keesha went on. "But it seems to me like real friends talk about stuff that's important. And you know what? I think that lately, you only talk about important stuff with Jeff. In fact, in the last month or so, Jeff's just about the only person you've had *any* time to talk to."

"Keesha, that's not *true*. Listen to me—" Nikki began, but Keesha opened her door and slid out.

"No, *you* listen. I made time for you today. That's what friends do. But every time I've tried to do anything with you for the past couple weeks, you've been too busy. Think about it, Nik. Just think about it."

❦ *Five* ❦

WHEN NIKKI PARKED the Mazda in her grandparents' driveway that afternoon, she had plenty on her mind. She got out, surprised at how cold the wind off Lake Michigan had become. She pulled the cardigan of her sweater set close around her and hurried to open the kitchen door. The meaty smell of roast chicken filled the kitchen, and she relaxed her shoulders in the welcome warmth of the room.

Gram looked up from the potato she was paring and smiled her welcome. Nikki smiled back and watched as Grandpa emptied the kitchen wastebasket, tugging at the overfilled white trash bag to lift it out. Gallie sidled up behind him, watching carefully in case any food dropped.

"Go on, boy." Grandpa nudged him gently to one side with his foot. "You're living up to your reputation as a trash hound, as usual." The bag came free suddenly, and Nikki grinned to hear Grandpa resume the absent-minded, tuneless whistling through his teeth that he usually carried on when he worked around the house.

Nikki dropped her backpack on the table and gave her grandmother a brief one-armed hug, then stole a chunk of raw potato from the pot.

"You!" Gram pointed the peeler at her. "Stop eating up all my work."

"Can't help it, Gram, I'm starving. Anybody call for me?"

34

Gram was peeling the potato again, her slender fingers moving in steady rhythm with the brown strips of peel falling into the sink. "Now, I wonder who you could mean by 'anybody'?" She looked up and winked at Nikki. "No, Jeff didn't call, honey. But your mother did. She wants you to call her back as soon as you can." She glanced at the kitchen clock. "You've got quite a while till I get these cooked and mashed."

Nikki stopped chewing, the potato still in her mouth. Rachel didn't normally call in the middle of the day, because her days were taken up with the music classes she taught at the junior college in Millbrook. "Did she say if anything happened? Like, with my dad or anything?"

Gram looked up and shook her head gently. "I don't think so, honey. It sounded like she just wanted to talk."

"Okay," Nikki said. "I'll call her from upstairs, then. I have to go up to my room and get something warmer on, anyway. It's freezing out there."

Upstairs, she pulled open her bottom dresser drawer and unearthed heavy jeans and a sweatshirt from the winter before. She changed quickly, then sat down cross-legged on the bed and dialed Rachel Sheridan's number in Ohio.

"Mother?" she said, as soon as she heard Rachel's hello on the other end. "Gram said you wanted me to call you. Is everything okay there?"

"Hi, Nicole. Things are okay, but something happened here that I wanted to tell you about."

"Oh, yeah? What?"

"A student at the college named T.J. came by my office and asked for your phone number. He said he ran into you at the 7-Eleven this past weekend, and he really has to talk to you."

Nikki fell back on the bed, the phone still against her ear, wishing with all her heart that she had never gone near that 7-Eleven. She hoped that at least he hadn't said anything about her hanging up on him.

"Nikki?" Rachel said. "*Nicole?* Are you still there?"

"I'm here," Nikki answered, pushing the hair back off her forehead and staring up at the ceiling.

"Well, are you going to tell me who this T.J. is? Someone important? Or just somebody who fell head over heels in love when he saw you at the 7-Eleven?" her mother asked, laughing.

Nikki winced. *How on earth do I answer that?* She remembered telling her mother T.J.'s name once—in the middle of the horrible fight they'd had on the morning Rachel discovered she was pregnant. But it was obvious, from the way her mother was teasing, that she didn't remember.

Nikki wondered how Rachel would react if she told her the truth right now. After all the terrible things that had happened between Nikki and her parents as a result of the pregnancy, Nikki couldn't bring herself to just blurt it out. She tried to sidestep the question instead.

"Did he say what he wanted?" she asked.

"Not exactly. He seems quite the charming young man, Nikki." Rachel's last words were gently teasing, with just the hint of a question, but they set off another wave of anger at T.J.

Charming—that's putting it mildly! Nikki closed her eyes, seeing his blond hair and soccer jersey again. T.J. had been her first serious crush, and she'd watched adoringly for two years as his soccer exploits made him the darling of the school. He'd always looked right through her, though. At least until the day he stopped by her locker and, with no explanation, asked her to meet him after his soccer match. She'd been close to speechless, yet tried to sound as nonchalant as though these kinds of invitations came her way every day, all the while knowing she would willingly have died rather than turn him down.

What an idiot I was! she thought, looking back with disgust at the person she'd been. *I couldn't even see through the most obvious ploy in the world—T.J. acting like he cared about me when all he wanted was—*

"Nicole! Excuse me, but I'm starting to feel as though I'm having this conversation alone!"

Rachel's words brought her back to the present. "I'm sorry, Mother. What was that you said?"

"I gave up trying to get information about the mysterious T.J., and I was telling you that the Bible study group decided to meet here from now on, at the house. But your mind is obviously on something else! Somebody better tell Jeff to watch out, maybe, hmmm?" Rachel laughed easily as she talked, and Nikki thought once again how different this conversation would have been just two months ago.

Then suddenly, in mid-sentence, Rachel's voice turned serious, and she sounded as though something had knocked the breath out of her. "Nikki? I—I just thought of something. I—well, I may not be right about this, but—" She took a deep breath and began again. "I'm trying to remember the name of the boy you said was Evan's— father."

Nikki was silent. It was impossible to speak through the tightness in her throat.

"Oh, Nikki. Honey? I'm so sorry I teased you about T.J. I should have put two and two together. I should have at least remembered his name!"

The words Nikki squeezed out finally were little more than a hoarse whisper. "It's okay, Mom. We weren't listening to each other very well back in those days, were we?"

"No, we weren't." Rachel's voice sounded sad, and they were both quiet for a moment. Then she asked, "Nikki? He asked for your phone number—"

Nikki considered this for a moment. Her first response was to shout, "No! Don't *ever* give him my phone number!" But something in her almost relished the thought of telling T.J. what she really thought of him. "I don't know, Mother. Right now that doesn't seem like such a good idea, but let me think about it. Listen, I'm gonna go now, okay?"

She hung up the phone and went on staring at the ceiling, her eyes fixed on the spot where she'd swatted a mosquito that had plagued her throughout one hot, endless July night. The mosquito had dried, forgotten, where she'd squashed it, and her eyes traced the outline of it on the ceiling above her, over and over, as she lay there hating T.J.

Charming. That's what Rachel had called him.

Oh, he's charming, all right, Nikki thought, *until you get to know what he's really like.*

She kept her eyes wide open, and still the pictures played in front of her—pictures of T.J. and what they'd done the night she got pregnant. And pictures of him walking out of the bedroom with hardly a backward glance when it was all over, to go on drinking with his friends in the family room as though nothing had even happened.

There were more pictures, too. Pictures of a T.J. so drunk friends had to drive him home, and of Nikki leaving the party much later that night, walking the six blocks home, alone and scared. There were pictures of her watching for T.J. in the halls at school in the weeks that followed, as worry began nagging at her day after day. Worry that something new was happening in her body, something different from anything she'd ever experienced. The pictures switched back to T.J., who was always surrounded by friends, always avoiding Nikki's eyes. And in those pictures, he was always laughing, while she was crying her nights away.

The pictures changed again, back to Nikki at the clinic, alone, trying to handle by herself the news the nurse had just given her, the news that she was pregnant. But Nikki had no intention of going there.

Not now! she thought. *Not after all I've been through.*

She swung herself up to a standing position on the bed and swiped her pillow at the mosquito with all her might, dislodging it. The brittle, weightless body drifted slowly to the comforter. Nikki picked it up gingerly with thumb and forefinger, her lips curled with distaste as she dropped it into the wastebasket.

Wouldn't it be wonderful, she thought as she watched the thread-like body and gossamer wings float downward and settle delicately on a bed of crumpled pink tissues, *if I could get rid of T.J. that way?*

As she turned to leave the bedroom, she realized with shock that somehow her original desire—to learn how to forgive and get beyond what had happened in the last year and a half—had actually turned into a desire to get rid of T.J.

∞

That evening, after Nikki helped Gram load the dishwasher and wipe the counters and scour the sink, she sat at the kitchen table trying to decipher a Spanish essay she was supposed to translate. It was harder to concentrate here in the middle of the kitchen, but more than anything Nikki wanted to avoid being alone with her thoughts right now.

At the other end of the table Gram was paring apples for the pie filling she canned every autumn, and Nikki glanced up to watch her work. Curling red peels dropped to rest on the newspaper Gram had spread to protect the tabletop, and the room began to fill with the sweet, fruity scent.

Gram looked up to find her watching, and smiled. "You won't get much done watching me."

"Yeah, I know," Nikki answered. "I've been sitting here trying to figure out this word so I wouldn't have to go upstairs and get the Spanish dictionary. Guess I'll have to, though."

A few minutes later, as she was pulling the dictionary off the shelf in her bedroom, the phone rang. Nikki went to the hall table and picked it up.

"Nik? It's Jeff. What are you doing?"

Nikki smiled at the sound of his voice. "Nothing important. Just some Spanish homework." She took the phone back into her bedroom, shut the door, and curled up on the window seat.

He gave her the details of his day, and asked about hers. Nikki told him about the vandalism at the high school.

"You're kidding. That kind of language has to be a new low, even for graffiti."

"It's kind of unbelievable, isn't it?"

"Well, a few years ago, it would've been," Jeff answered. "But after all the school violence in the last couple of years, it doesn't shock you quite so much. I just hope it stops with graffiti. I'd hate to see anybody get hurt. Like *you*."

The corners of Nikki's mouth curved up in a smile. It still caught her off guard, that feeling of sudden pleasure that sometimes shot through her at just a word from Jeff.

"Hey," he murmured, his voice low. "Still there?"

"Yeah, I'm here," she said, leaning her head against the cool glass of the windowpane.

"You're smiling. I can hear it," he said.

"Sometimes that happens when I talk to you, now, doesn't it?" Nikki answered.

"Oh, yeah? Wish I was there so you could tell me all about it."

They talked back and forth for several minutes, saying nothing in particular, and at the same time, saying everything.

Nikki felt as though she was talking and listening with one part of herself, while at the same time standing back and watching the whole conversation with wonder. *I can't believe we're sitting here talking like this, after everything that's happened between us this past year.*

Her thoughts flashed back to the summer a year before, when Jeff had wanted so much to be there for her, and she'd pushed him away. And then to this past summer, when she'd finally realized what she had lost by doing so. She'd longed with all her heart to have him back, and had felt heartsick for all the long months when it looked as though that could never happen.

And now, unaccountably, it had. Nikki breathed a long sigh of contentment and another half hour went by faster than she could have believed.

At last Jeff said, "Well listen, our talking this long isn't helping you get your Spanish done. I shouldn't keep you on the phone all night."

"Who cares about Spanish?" Nikki said.

"You do, that's who," Jeff answered. "Or at least you will, when grades come out. Keep that average up, lady, and you too can come and slave your life away at U of M!"

"I wish you were here," she said.

"Me, too. But listen, I will be, on Friday."

"You can make it this weekend? Oh, Jeff, I can't wait!"

"That's what I called to tell you, originally. We just got talking about all the other stuff—"

"I know. That's okay." There wasn't really anything else to say, but Nikki was reluctant to end the conversation, and she could tell Jeff felt the same way Having a phone wire connect them was not nearly enough, but it was better than nothing.

The next few days were filled with homework and classes. Hollis and Noel said little to Nikki except for quick "hellos" when they walked past her desk in Current Events class. Much of the hall conversation at school was still speculation as to who had spray-painted the graffiti on the walls. Everybody, it seemed, had a theory—but most of them sounded nonsensical to Nikki.

She shared them with Jeff during their nightly phone calls, along with all the other news of each day. On Thursday night they'd been talking for an hour or so when Nikki stopped suddenly.

"Hey," she asked, "isn't this the night you're supposed to go to that Intervarsity meeting?"

"Yeah. So?"

"Well, why didn't you go?" she demanded.

" 'Cuz I'd rather be talking to you," he answered.

"Jeff!" she said, as though scolding him. But inside, his words made her smile.

"I'll go next week, don't worry," Jeff said. Then he added, "Unless I'm talking to you, that is."

"What'd you say?" Nikki asked. "Sirens just went off outside and I can hardly hear you."

"Sirens? In Rosendale?" Jeff laughed. "I didn't even know they had sirens there."

"Well, listen," Nikki said reluctantly, "I hate to say this, but I better go. Somebody's been trying to call in for the last five minutes. I keep hearing the clicks."

It took another few minutes, but they finally said good-bye and Nikki switched to the other call.

"Nikki! I didn't think you'd *ever* get off the phone! I've been calling you forever!" Keesha's voice was breathless.

Nikki tried to explain she'd been talking with Jeff, but Keesha talked right over her.

"Nikki, would you listen to me? The school's on fire!"

❧ *Six* ❧

"*WHAT* SCHOOL?" Nikki asked.

"*Our* school, of course! The high school! There's a fire in the side wing, by the chemistry lab. Go turn on your TV—they're doing live coverage. They're calling in fire departments from all the towns around here and everything!"

Nikki ran downstairs to the living room as Keesha talked. The noise of the sirens now made sense. She searched the coffee table and end tables for the remote, then gave up and switched on the TV manually. Sure enough, just to the left of the Howellsville High School sign, a reporter stood silhouetted against a background of glowing orange flames.

"Do you see it? Have you got the TV on?" Keesha kept asking.

"Yeah, Keesha. Hold on a minute, would you?"

Nikki covered the mouthpiece with her hand. "Gram! Grandpa! Come here—in the living room!" She uncovered the phone. "Keesha, I can't believe this—that's the chemistry lab!"

The Channel 16 news camera moved in for a close-up shot. Nikki watched, open-mouthed, as flames spurted out of a lab window and licked up the sides of the brick building. Firemen were everywhere, it seemed, holding huge hoses that poured streams of water into the blaze.

Nikki lowered herself onto the hassock, never taking her eyes off

42

the screen, and shook her head slowly as she watched the water pour into the flames. "Even if they do get the fire out, the whole lab'll be ruined from the water."

"You're probably right, honey," Grandpa agreed from where he and Gram now stood behind her. He laid both hands on her shoulders and squeezed gently as they watched.

On the phone, Keesha was talking on and on, in her excitement repeating everything the reporter said, and adding her own comments.

"It appears that someone broke into the lab and used some of the chemicals there to intensify the fire," the reporter said, her words tumbling out rapidly as though she, too, was near panic. "Officials say it's unlikely the fire could have burned this hot and fast otherwise." She turned and glanced nervously at the flames behind her, as though she'd like to edge forward, farther from the heat.

"Then it's certain that the fire was set?" the anchorman asked.

The reporter held a finger to the microphone in her ear, as though to hear better, then looked back into the camera. "I don't think anything's 'certain' yet, John. That's just what we're hearing from people here. It's probably just speculation at this point. But we do have to take into account that this fire has occurred only days after the spray-painting incident. That definitely puts this fire in the suspicious category."

"Oh, man, Nik, did you hear that?" Keesha said, as Channel 16 broke for commercials. "Somebody broke in and *set* the fire. Who do you think would've done it? I mean, you'd have to be really *crazy* to do that and think you could get away with it." She paused to take a breath, but just barely. "Remember that school shooting out west? Where the kid who did it was mad because he got kicked off the basketball team? Do we know anybody who got kicked off one of the teams? Or suspended or anything?"

"Keesha! Take a breath, would you?" Nikki finally broke in, exasperated.

"But, Nik! How can you be so calm when the whole school's burning to the ground? And we might be able to figure out who—"

"Stop, Keesha. The whole school's *not* burning to the ground. It's just one room, and it's only connected to the main building by that one hallway. I mean, what's happening is bad enough, but don't make it sound worse than it is. They probably won't even cancel school tomorrow."

"You're kidding! I figured we'd get out of classes for at least a week over this."

"Right. Dream on," Nikki told her, laughing a little at Keesha's dramatics in spite of herself.

"Okay, then, at least for a day. Listen, Nik, you want to drive over and see the fire for real? Not just on TV, I mean. We could park up on the street, you know, away from the fire trucks—"

"No way, Keesha. Besides, we can probably see better on TV . . ." She broke off as the reporter appeared on the screen again. The sound cut back in during the middle of the conversation between the anchorman and the reporter.

"Yes, John, we do have confirmation from the police that there had been a threat made," the reporter said.

"Can you tell us what the threat was?"

The reporter shook her head. "No, John, there's no specifics available yet about what was actually said."

"How was the threat made?" the news anchor asked.

"It was phoned in to the police station just about half an hour ago. They tell us the call's been traced back to a pay phone, but they won't say where," the reporter answered.

"And do you have any leads on who might have made that call?" the anchor asked.

"Not yet. All the police said was that the voice had been disguised—"

The rest was lost to Nikki. The reporter's words rang over and over in her ears, "the voice had been disguised . . . the voice had been disguised . . ."

The picture of a face flashed through Nikki's mind, the face of the one person she knew who often disguised his voice, but she pushed the thought away. *He would never do anything this crazy. Would he?*

In the end, Keesha got her wish. School was canceled on Friday.

The science room was heavily damaged and would need extensive repairs, but it could be blocked off from the rest of the school. The smoke and water damage was confined to that one area, and officials announced that most classes would resume on Monday. Nikki was upset about the damage, but delighted to get an extra day off.

"I can get all my homework done today," she told Grandpa over a leisurely breakfast of pancakes and bacon on Friday morning. "That way, Jeff and I can spend all our time together once he gets here tonight."

Grandpa sipped his coffee, then set his cup down deliberately. "Seems like you and Jeff are pretty much doing that already. Even when he isn't here, you're on the phone together."

Nikki pulled her velour robe close around her and snuggled her cold toes farther into her fuzzy slippers. "If you need the phone, just tell us and we'll be glad to get off—" she began.

Grandpa shook his head. "That's not really my point, honey. I'm just getting a little concerned about the two of you. I know you have homework, and music practice, and friends to keep up with. And Jeff has the same on his end, I'm sure."

Nikki smiled in relief. "Oh, hey, if that's what you're worried about, it's no problem. Jeff and I are both doing great in our classes." She got up and put her dishes in the dishwasher, then spun around like a dancer till she stood behind her grandfather's chair. She leaned down to hug him. "Can you believe things finally worked out for Jeff and me, Grandpa? Don't you think it's *great?*"

She turned toward her grandmother, who was bringing more pancakes to the table, and was struck by the sudden realization that she was leaving much more of the housework to Gram these days. "I'm going back upstairs right now and get all my homework done before lunch. Then I'll make those reuben sandwiches you like for your lunch, okay?"

∽

At lunchtime, Nikki was piling sauerkraut on the reubens when Keesha called.

"Nik! You wanna go to the mall in Grand Rapids this afternoon?" she asked. "My aunt's here and she says she'll watch Serena."

"I'm sorry, Keesha. I just called and made an appointment to get my hair highlighted this afternoon. Jeff's coming tonight, you know, and I want it to look really special."

Keesha sighed. "So that means you can't do anything this evening, either?"

"Keesha, I'm *sorry!* But I just told you, *Jeff's* coming," Nikki answered.

There was silence for a few seconds while Nikki spooned the last of the sauerkraut onto the sandwiches. Then she asked, "Keesha? You're still there, aren't you?"

"Yeah. I'm here."

"You could come with me while I get my hair done," Nikki offered.

"And sit around and watch? I don't think so. I wanted us to *do* something fun. *Together.*"

"Okay, so we will," Nikki said, determined not to let Keesha spoil her happiness at Jeff's coming. "Next week sometime, all right?"

"I guess some people are just too busy to be friends," Keesha said, her voice quiet.

Nikki set the saucepan back on the stove with a thump. "Keesha, that's not fair and you know it! The only time Jeff and I ever get to see each other is on weekends."

"Right. I understand."

Keesha sounded so lonely that Nikki nearly called her back, but the sandwiches had to be eaten right away or all her work would be wasted.

She turned toward the hall. "Gram! Grandpa! Lunch's ready!"

❦ *Seven* ❧

BY 6:00 THAT EVENING, Nikki was back from her hair appointment and standing in front of the wavy old dresser mirror in her bedroom, surveying her reflection. The hairdresser had trimmed a good two inches off her hair, which left it just long enough to brush gracefully against the shoulders of her rose-colored sweater. The new gold highlights the hairdresser had put in caught the light and gave her hair a soft glow.

She held her hands up in front of her and admired her nails, painted a dusky rose to match her sweater. She'd decided at the last minute to splurge and have them done at the beauty shop, and she was pleased now that she'd spent the money. She looked at herself in the mirror and grinned.

"Nails like a *model!* Way to go, Nik!" she congratulated her reflection. For years she'd struggled to stop peeling off her nails whenever she got nervous, and conquering the habit had pleased her no end. She laughed at her own silliness, then hugged herself impulsively. It was actually beginning to look as though some things were finally, *finally*, beginning to go well for her again.

The phone rang and Nikki dashed to the phone table in the hall.

"Hello. Uh, may I speak with—with Nikki? Nikki Sheridan?"

Nikki stood absolutely still, trying to place who was speaking, and felt her stomach knot up as she recognized T.J.'s voice.

"Hello?" the voice came again. "Is this the right number? Is anybody there?"

Nikki swallowed hard, then demanded, "How did you get my number? Who told you—wait a minute! Did my *mother* give you this number?"

"Hey! Hold on here. And don't hang up this time!" T.J. said quickly. Nikki had the impression he was keeping his voice casual only with great effort. "You don't have to get so upset. Your mother and I were talking and I told her I really wanted to get in touch with you. Can't you just talk to me for a minute?"

"I have nothing to say to you, T.J."

"Nikki—"

"Nothing, T.J. *Nothing.* Can I *possibly* make that any clearer?"

"Nikki, come on! You act like we never even went out together. We were friends, remember? I just want to ask you a question. See, what you said on Saturday, in the 7-Eleven, got me thinking—"

Nikki pushed the TALK button and set the phone down deliberately. Her first impulse was to call her mother and pour out her fury—to tell her in no uncertain terms what she thought of Rachel's giving T.J. her phone number. *And after I asked you not to!* she fumed. But she knew she couldn't talk to Rachel now, not in this frame of mind. Not after they'd come this far in their relationship. *I'll call her tomorrow. Or later tonight, when I've settled down.*

Nikki returned to her room and positioned herself in front of the mirror again. She tried to recapture the excitement she'd felt, that sense that things were finally turning around for her, but T.J.'s call had chased the feeling far away.

Instead, she found herself pacing back and forth between the bed and the dresser, trying to stem the flow of memories that threatened to drown her.

I don't have to think about all this again. Evan's been adopted. He's settled in a good home. The whole situation's over and done with. T.J. has no right to butt into my life this way. She stopped and found herself in front of the mirror again and leaned forward, bracing her hands on the edge of the dresser. "And there's absolutely no way I'm telling you about Evan, T.J.!"

Nikki heard the wheels of Jeff's Bronco crunch over the gravel in the driveway between her grandparents' house and the Allens' summer home. She straightened her sweater and reapplied her lipstick, then took a determined breath. She'd been waiting all week to see Jeff, and she wasn't about to let T.J. spoil this evening. She forced her mouth into a smile, then ran down the steps and to the kitchen door. Jeff and his family had been close to Nikki's grandparents for years, and in western Michigan, good friends rarely used the front door.

Jeff was waiting at the kitchen door. He took one look at Nikki, stepped inside and stretched both arms out to the sides. Nikki ran into them and he lifted her off her feet and spun her around.

"So hello, Gorgeous," he said at last as he set her gently back on the floor. Gallie was doing his best to nose in between them, wagging his feathery tail so hard his hindquarters swayed. Jeff rubbed the dog's golden head, then looked across the room to where Gram and Grandpa sat at the table watching the local news on the small kitchen TV. "Is it just my eyes," Jeff asked, "or does Nikki look especially terrific tonight?"

"It better not be your eyes, not after all she spent to look that way," Grandpa murmured with a little grin.

"Oh, thanks, Grandpa! Give away all my secrets, why don't you?" Nikki joked.

They all laughed together, but Nikki noted that Gram's smile seemed a bit strained. *That's strange*, Nikki thought. *I wonder what's bothering her?*

Nikki glanced at the TV screen, and a picture of the school fire the night before flashed across it. She held up one hand to stop the others from talking. "Hey, listen for just a minute. They're talking about the fire again."

"What fire?" Jeff asked, but Nikki hushed him.

"I understand we've learned the nature of the threat that was phoned in last night at the time of the fire, is that correct?" the anchorwoman was asking.

"That's true," the reporter said. "A reliable source close to the Howellsville police department tells us that the caller apparently only spoke for a few seconds. He—or she—we can't really tell until the final voice analysis is made—said only seven words: 'This time the building. Next time, people.'"

"That's a chilling statement, don't you think?" the anchor asked. "What plans does the school have to protect the students?"

"It is chilling, you're absolutely right. Police have been meeting with Howellsville school board members all afternoon, and they're putting together a plan that may include banning all but see-through backpacks, and posting armed guards to check students at the doors. There've been so many instances of school violence across the country that safety procedures are pretty well established."

"And now it comes to Howellsville. Hard to believe, isn't it?" the anchor said, shaking her head before going on to the next news item.

"Whoa," Nikki said, hitting the MUTE button. "Can you believe this?"

Jeff pulled up a chair and straddled it, folding his arms across the back. "I think you better fill me in here. The last I heard, there was some graffiti. Now there's fires? And threats?"

"Remember last night? When I told you I couldn't hear what you said because of the sirens? Well, there was a fire at the high school, in the science lab. It did enough damage that they had to close school today, but they're saying we'll be back in classes on Monday."

"How can you go back in that fast?"

"You've seen the high school, right?" Nikki asked, and Jeff nodded. "You know that part of the building that juts out to the left? That's where the lab was, and they'll just block that all off while they rebuild it. There's not much there except the lab and restrooms. And the janitor's closet. We'll just use the rest of the building."

Jeff frowned. "And they think it was arson?"

Nikki nodded. "That's what it sounds like. Why?"

"Well, don't you think that if somebody wanted to burn down the school, they would've started the fire where it could do more damage to the whole building?"

She considered for a moment. "Maybe, but they said on the news that they did it in the lab so they could use chemicals. You know, make a hotter fire that would move faster and do a lot more damage.

But I guess somebody called the firemen before it spread too far."

Jeff rested his chin on his hands for a second, then straightened back up. "This is unbelievable. Nik, I'm not sure you're even safe going back there. And now, with this threat—it sounds like whoever did it means business." He turned to Nikki's grandparents. "Don't you think this sounds dangerous?"

Grandpa pushed back his chair and took his coffee cup to the sink. "I think all we can do is wait for the police to find out what's really going on. So far, there's only a suspicion of arson—it hasn't been proven. Whoever made the phone call could have done it as a prank—taking credit for something he or she didn't even do."

Jeff gave a half-shrug, but Nikki could tell he was unconvinced. "That may be true. But in the meantime, I think somebody needs to make sure no students get hurt."

"Oh, I think the community will see to it that the police do all they can." He crossed the room to stand behind his wife's chair, massaging her shoulders gently. He looked up. "So, Jeff, on a more pleasant note—how are your parents doing?"

By the time Jeff had covered all the news, Nikki was impatient to leave. She caught Jeff's eye and nodded toward the door when her grandparents weren't looking.

Jeff got to his feet and pushed the chair back into place. "Guess we'll get going, if that's okay with you."

Grandpa nodded and stood up, too. "You'll be okay tonight, Jeff? Staying over in your house alone there?"

"Oh, sure," Jeff said. "You know I've done it lots of times."

Grandpa rubbed the bridge of his nose with his forefinger and thumb, and his glasses slid up and down with the motion. "I didn't even get to ask how classes are going for you."

Jeff gave a short laugh. "Maybe that's better, sir. It wasn't exactly the best of weeks."

"I thought you usually do pretty well in school, Jeff," Grandpa said as they moved toward the door.

"Well, yeah, I do. I mean I *did*. I just don't seem to have as much time to get things done as I used to. I turned a paper in a little late this week, and the professor dropped the grade, no questions asked, no explanations allowed."

"It sounds as though you'll have to spend a little more time on homework and a lot less on the phone, hmm?" Gram said. "Anyway, you come on over for waffles tomorrow morning. About 9:30, 10:00. And Jeff—you be sure and take good care of our girl tonight."

Nikki looked at her grandmother in surprise. She'd never heard her address Jeff in that tone before.

"Well—sure. I mean, of course I will." Jeff, caught off guard, groped for words. "I'd never let anything happen to Nikki."

When they got into the red Bronco, Nikki automatically slid across the seat to snuggle up against Jeff, and he put his arm around her. "You'll have to shift for me, you know," he said, rubbing his chin against the top of her head. For an instant, the picture of T.J.'s face flashed through her mind, and she remembered him doing exactly the same thing when they used to go out. But she pushed the thought away immediately.

"Don't I always?" Nikki asked. She shifted into reverse and Jeff began backing out.

"Nik, did you feel a little bit like I was getting the third degree in there?" he asked as they reached the street and Nikki pushed it into first.

Nikki shrugged. "Yeah, I don't know what that was all about. Gram was acting weird, wasn't she?"

Jeff nodded. "Almost like she was afraid to let you go out with me or something."

"Up to now, I've always thought she trusted you more than she does me, so I don't have a clue. Anyway, where're we headed?"

Jeff glanced down at her. "Is Rosie's all right? I know it's not fancy, but—"

Nikki turned her head and rubbed her forehead against Jeff's cheek. "Hey, you don't have to apologize. You've been traveling all afternoon to get here. I don't expect you to drive anywhere far tonight."

"You know what, Nik? You're great," Jeff said, and pulled her closer. She snuggled against his side, but as she did so, the picture of T.J. flashed through her mind again, spoiling the moment. She closed her eyes to try to block it out, wondering if she could ever get past what had happened with him.

❦ *Eight* ❦

THE LIGHT WAS FADING quickly by the time they got to Rosie's. The small, squat stucco building looked forlorn beneath the faded pink ROSIE'S GRILL—BURGERS AND MALTS sign.

In the summer, Nikki thought, your eyes were immediately drawn away from the building to the wide, blue expanse of Lake Michigan beyond—or to the striped canvas beach umbrellas that flapped in the breeze over round, metal tables on the wide deck.

But tonight the gray of the October sky seemed to bring out the gray of the stained stucco walls. The bright umbrellas had long since been stored for winter.

"This place is starting to look pretty shabby, isn't it?" Jeff asked, as they walked together toward the door. The wind off Lake Michigan had become bitingly cold, and they hurried together to reach the shelter of the building.

"I was just thinking that. You don't notice as much in the summer, I guess," Nikki answered. Jeff pushed the door open and she walked through ahead of him. Mingled smells of burgers and burritos and hot grease enveloped them as they stood just inside the doorway for a moment, deciding where to sit. In the end they took a table by the windows that would have had a beautiful view of the lake, had it been light enough. This evening the view was totally gray. Even the water had taken on the color of the sky. Lights were already beginning to twinkle up and down the shoreline in the gathering darkness.

Nikki stared out at the lights as they waited for the waitress. She couldn't help thinking about the phone call she'd gotten just before Jeff arrived. *I hope that's the last time I ever have to talk to T.J.* Still, she couldn't help wondering what he had wanted. It had to be something about Evan. *If only I hadn't been so stupid and said that about pregnancy changing a person. When will I ever learn to keep my mouth shut?*

"*Beef* or *chicken?*" a voice asked, and Nikki realized that she'd just heard the same thing a second before. She looked up to see the waitress staring at her impatiently, then at Jeff, who was also watching her, and came back to the present.

"I told her you probably wanted a burrito," Jeff said, his eyebrows raised.

"Oh, yeah. I do. Chicken," she said. "And a Coke."

The waitress scribbled on her yellow pad, took Jeff's order also, then disappeared in the direction of the kitchen.

"Nice to have you back, Nik," Jeff said. He pushed aside the red-glass candle holder carefully, so as not to put out the flame, and reached across the table for her hands.

"I'm sorry. I was just thinking about—things." She hesitated, wondering if she dared mention T.J. to Jeff, then dismissed the thought and turned the conversation to safer territory. "There's a lot on my mind these days, like my parents and all."

Jeff squeezed her hands gently, then rubbed his thumbs back and forth over hers. "Have you talked to your father at all since he came up here to see you in September?"

"I tried to call him once, but I got the answering machine," she answered.

"Leave a message?"

She shook her head.

She didn't tell him how much it had hurt to hear the message on the answering machine. The voice had been Madeleine's—the young daughter of the woman her father was living with, the daughter she'd heard him call 'Maddie'.

"Mother hasn't been able to talk to him, either, I guess. You know how I told you she's in that prayer group now? She said they pray for him, and the pastor at the church tried to get him to come to counseling with her, but he won't even return her calls."

The burritos came then, steaming hot. Nikki closed her eyes and inhaled, glad to change the subject. "Mmm, they smell wonderful, don't they?"

Jeff seemed to sense her feelings, as he did so often now, and changed the subject. "So you got the whole day off, huh? Must be nice! What'd you do with all your spare time?"

"Nothing exciting, believe me." She told him about her appointment at the hairdresser, and about finishing up her homework so they could have more time together.

He winked across the table at her when she said that, then sighed. "I'll tell you what, *I* could a use a whole day off. I might actually catch up on a couple of papers I have due."

"Oh, right," Nikki teased. "You're the one who's always ahead of the game, at least in the homework department. I seem to remember Carly getting really steamed at you a couple times over that, don't I?"

"Yeah," Jeff laughed, remembering. "That always did bug her, didn't it? She used to finish her math papers at the breakfast table, a pencil in one hand and a spoon in the other." His face turned serious. "But I'm not doing so well in that department right now, myself. I just seem to always be short of time these days."

Nikki felt a sudden pang of guilt and thought of what her grandmother had said. "We're spending a lot of time on the phone, Jeff. Do you think that's making things worse?"

Jeff wiped his mouth with his napkin and shook his head. "Hey, a guy's gotta have time for the important things in life." He put his napkin down and reached again for her free hand. "And I definitely put you in the 'important things' category, Nicole Sheridan. Right at the top of the list."

Nikki looked into his dark blue eyes and thought how much she'd like him to kiss her, then and there. But the warm glow subsided almost immediately as the thought brought back the memory of a time when she'd had exactly the same feelings about T.J.— memories she'd thought were long buried. *I wanted T.J. to kiss me, too. My feelings for him were just this strong, once, and look where that landed me. Pregnant.*

A wave of fear washed over Nikki. She tried to pretend she didn't feel it. *I would never let Jeff do what T.J. did,* she told herself. *Besides, Jeff wouldn't even try.* But it didn't help. She couldn't get around remembering that she had once thought exactly the same thing about T. J.

"Nikki. *Nikki.*" Jeff's voice was insistent as his fingers tightened on hers. "What's going on tonight, Nik? You're dreaming on me again."

Nikki had just opened her mouth to apologize when the door opened. From the noise, Nik could tell without turning around that it was a whole group. She finished the last bite of her burrito while they waited for the screech of chairs on the tile floor and loud laughing to subside.

At last, when things were quieter, she tried again. "Jeff, I'm sorry I keep daydreaming." But now it was Jeff who wasn't paying attention. He was staring at something over her shoulder, and she turned to see what. Chad Davies was there, along with four of his friends from school and a few other guys she'd never seen. A couple of them had pulled two tables together and positioned extra chairs around them, which accounted for all the noise. The others clustered around Chad, cheering him on where he stood playing one of the arcade games. Nikki groaned inwardly, remembering the confrontation over her that Jeff and Chad had had the winter before.

She had the uncomfortable feeling that, though she'd stopped going out with Chad half a year ago, he still thought he had some say in her life. His words in Current Events class on Monday morning came back to her, about getting together with her, about his opinion of Jeff. *We need to get out of here before Chad sees Jeff and starts mouthing off,* she thought, wiping her mouth and fingers quickly with her napkin.

Jeff's eyes narrowed. "Don't I know that guy—the blond one playing the video game? I just can't think where I met him."

Nikki sighed. "Remember last year, when I was all messed up? And I was dating a guy named Chad?"

Recognition dawned in Jeff's eyes. "Oh, brother. It's all coming back to me!"

"Uh-huh. Well, it'd probably be better if we didn't end up talking to him right now." Nikki wadded up her napkin and set it down beside her plate. "What do you say we go home now, Jeff?" She slid her chair back a few inches, but Jeff shook his head.

"What's the problem here, Nik? You act like you're scared of this guy or something."

"Not scared. It just pays to be careful around him. I mean, he used to have a hair trigger temper, when I was going out with him last year. But now he's really hard to read. Like on Sunday—remember I told you how I nearly saw an accident on Sunday?"

"You mean he was the one you were telling me about, who ran the stop sign?" Jeff broke in. "You didn't say it was him!"

Nikki nodded. "Yeah, well, the whole thing was pretty crazy. He ran the stop sign and just kept going like nothing even happened. I'm worried he might be drinking again." She thought back to his sudden anger in class. "He's just acting weird. One minute he's fine, then the next he explodes over something. You never really know where a conversation with him is gonna go these days."

Twin red spots appeared over Jeff's cheekbones, always a sure sign he was upset. "Are you telling me he loses his temper at *you?*"

Nikki considered his question. "No, not exactly. Actually, he can be really nice to me. It's just weird, though, the way his mood changes—" she snapped her fingers in the space between them "—like that!"

"Nikki, it sounds like maybe I *should* talk to him. He can't go around running stop signs and having temper tantrums. What if he hurts somebody—like you, for instance?"

Nikki covered Jeff's hand with hers and squeezed her thank-you, but shook her head at the same time. "You don't understand. Chad's been through some really rough things in the last couple years with his family. Sometimes he just seems so angry and bitter, and other days he looks really depressed."

Jeff looked skeptical. "Nikki, you sound like you're trying to, like, look out for him. You're not still—still—"

Nikki couldn't help but grin for a second. "Jeff Allen, are you trying to say you're jealous? Of Chad?"

He raised one eyebrow at her, but didn't answer. Nikki squeezed his hand. "You don't ever have to worry about Chad, Jeff. Not that way. But I worry about him because he's been through a lot . . . His mother left. And his dad handles it by getting—and staying—drunk, apparently. He was some big executive, but he lost his job because of the drinking, and that's why they moved here. I get the feeling Chad ends up taking care of him—and just about everything else at home—these days."

"He's the one who hit Gallie and broke his leg, isn't he?"

"Right." Nikki winced at the memory, and at the part she'd played in the situation. "Remember your dad told him about an alcoholism treatment place last year? I think Chad tried to get his father to go, but I don't know if he ever did or not. So, anyway, can we just stop talking history and leave now? I don't want you to see his temper firsthand, that's all."

Jeff signaled the waitress and paid the bill, and they headed toward the door. They were almost there when Chad turned to speak to one of his friends and caught sight of Nikki. He stepped away from the video game, coming toward her.

"Nikki!" He said her name in exaggerated tones, as though greeting a long-lost friend. "Nikki, sweetheart—oh, *excuse* me. I thought you were alone. I didn't see your friend there." He peered at Jeff more closely, and seemed slightly unsteady on his feet. "Wait a minute," he went on now, staring at Jeff. "I know you—you're the one used to hang around Nikki's all the time. Preacher, isn't that what I used to call you?"

He turned to the others and jerked his head in Jeff's direction, the shock of nearly white-blond hair falling back from his forehead. "Hey, you guys need to meet somebody here—"

The guys at the table paid little attention to Chad's words. "Leave him alone, Chad," one called out, his voice bored.

"No, man. You gotta meet him. He's one of Nikki's *very special* boyfriends." He looked down at her and smirked.

Jeff seemed unfazed by Chad's talk. Whereas Nikki's only desire was to get out of there, fast, he closed the distance between himself and Chad with two deliberate steps, putting their faces just inches apart.

"I'm not a preacher, but I *am* a Christian. Is there something you want to say to me about that?" Jeff's voice was quiet, but he leaned forward a little as he waited, purposely invading Chad's space.

Chad took one step back involuntarily, and Nikki could tell he'd been caught off guard. Jeff immediately moved forward to close the space. "Because if you do, I want you to know I'm listening. Now's your chance."

There was total silence in Rosie's for a few seconds, and all eyes were on Chad. He tried to laugh it off, swaggering a bit as though Jeff didn't intimidate him at all. "Hey, don't go getting so steamed. I was just having a little fun."

Nikki was amazed at how easygoing Jeff sounded when he spoke again, but she sensed steel behind his words. "Well, now, let me tell it to you straight, Chad. I don't mind too much if you have a little fun at my expense." He took another step forward and Chad matched it with a step backward. "As long as you don't go having your fun at Nikki's expense. Who she goes out with is her own business. Understand?"

"I don't know what you're talking about, man—" Chad began, but Jeff cut him off.

"I hear you have a slight tendency to be a little short-tempered these days, maybe even run a stop sign now and then. I don't want to hear about any more of that, either. Got that?"

Nikki moved to Jeff's side and touched his forearm gently.

"Jeff," she whispered, "let's go now, okay?"

He glanced down at her and smiled, then looked back at Chad. "It's been great to see you again, Chad. Just don't forget anything I said, hmm?"

Chad jerked his head toward the door, as though willing Jeff gone.

"I'll take that as a 'yes,' " Jeff said. "Glad to know we agree." He put his hand under Nikki's elbow and steered her gently toward the door.

Nikki hadn't realized how long she'd been holding her breath until that moment. She took in a great gulp of air, and the two of them turned and walked out the door to the parking lot.

When they reached the Bronco, Jeff walked Nikki around to the passenger side and opened the door. But before she got in, he put both hands on her shoulders. "Listen, Nikki, you need to watch out for that guy. You let me know if he gives you any trouble, you hear?"

"Oh, right! And watch the two of you fight it out right in front of me!"

"Listen, I don't go around starting fights, Nik, you know that. On the other hand, I won't stand by and do nothing if he gives you a rough time, either." He slid his arms around her and pulled her close, holding her tightly for a moment. When he spoke, his words were nearly muffled against her hair. "Don't you understand, Nikki? I love you."

Nikki pulled back and stared up at his face. "Did you—did you just say what I think you said?"

In the glow of the streetlight, she could see his smile, uncertain at first, then more confident. "Yeah. I guess I did." He glanced around the parking lot, then at the stucco building. "This isn't exactly where I planned to say it, but it's true. I love you, Nikki Sheridan."

✣ *Nine* ✣

IT WAS NEARLY 10:00 when Nikki and Jeff arrived back at her grandparents' house. They'd driven into Howellsville and browsed through CDs at Circuit City, looking for one they could send to Carly. Then, since they were just down the road from the high school, they drove past it. Aside from the white wooden sawhorses and yellow tape that roped off the wing where the science room was located, there was no evidence of the fire.

They ordered drinks at the Burger King drive-up, then sat in the car and talked for another hour. As far as Nikki was concerned, the drinks and shopping mattered not at all. Being with Jeff was what counted. She wished they could prolong the evening forever.

The blue clapboard house was quiet when she finally opened the kitchen door and went inside. "Gram and Grandpa must have gone upstairs," she said over her shoulder to Jeff. "They're usually in bed by this time."

He stepped through the doorway and closed the door softly behind him. The tiny, shaded lamp on the kitchen counter that Gram used as a night light filled the room with a dim glow. In its light Jeff seemed taller than ever, and his closeness and the smell of his cologne made her heart beat faster.

Nikki looked up at him, and for a long minute they stood staring into each other's eyes. Over and over, like a magical chant in her mind, she heard, *Jeff loves me, Jeff loves me, Jeff loves me!* When he reached out his arms to help her take off her coat, it seemed only natural to move closer to him, and the first thing she knew they were kissing in a way they never had before.

Time had nothing to do with them, it seemed, as they stood with their arms tight around each other. She was only aware of the sweetness of Jeff's lips on hers and the chant of his love in her mind.

When the kitchen light overhead snapped on suddenly, it was as though a dream shattered in the glare. Nikki and Jeff jerked backwards, away from each other, and turned to see who was there.

Gram stood perfectly still in the doorway, her old, white chenille robe belted loosely around her, the shawl collar embroidered with pink flowers and vines, a few pulled threads dangling from the ends of the tie belt. Her hand was still on the light switch, and her face wore a look of shock.

The tension in the room was almost palpable, and no one seemed to know what to do to break it. Finally Gram's hand dropped from the light switch and she took a step forward, her eyes troubled.

"I didn't realize you were home," she said at last.

Nikki gave a nervous laugh. "Yeah, well, we, uh, we just got back. Just a minute ago." She glanced at Jeff as though for help. "Didn't we, Jeff? We've been here like—I don't know—maybe three or four minutes."

She looked at Jeff again, willing him to enter the conversation—to say something, anything, to help smooth over this awkward minute. But Jeff stood absolutely still, staring down at his feet. Nikki turned back to Gram.

"So—you couldn't sleep?" she asked brightly.

Gram moved toward the refrigerator, nodding. "I thought maybe some hot milk would help."

"I'm really sorry if we kept you up—"

Gram glanced back over her shoulder with a look that squelched all Nikki's attempts to smooth over the tension. "You *didn't* keep me up, not before. But you may now."

At that, Jeff moved uneasily toward the door. "I guess I better go," he said. Nikki tried to smile at him, but her smile felt tight and unnatural.

"Yeah. I'll see you tomorrow," she said.

Nikki said a quick good night and went upstairs, breathing a sigh of relief that Gram had not stopped her. She slipped her arms through the sleeves of her soft velour robe and tied the belt around her. She was just about to curl up on the window seat with her journal and try to recapture the magic she'd felt earlier when there was a knock on the door.

"Nikki?" her grandmother's voice called. Nikki winced and crossed to open the door.

Carole Nobles pulled her own robe closer around her. "I'd like to talk to you for a moment, Nikki. May I come in?"

Nikki nodded and stepped back to let her grandmother pass. "Would you like the window seat, Gram?" she asked.

"Oh, maybe I'd better stick with the bed here," Carole said, patting the side of Nikki's bed as she sat down. Nikki went back to the window seat and sat close to the edge, dreading what was coming. *We weren't doing anything wrong*, she thought, defensiveness rising inside her. *It's not like we were doing something immoral. Everybody kisses.* Thoughts raced through her head, thoughts of things she could say when Gram started in on her.

Gram, however, only looked across the room at her and smiled. "Your hair looks beautiful, honey. I didn't get to tell you before, with all the news about the fire, and with Jeff coming and all. Oh, and I almost forgot—your mother called and left a message for you to call her. She says she's having trouble getting through to you. That the line's almost always busy. Funny thing is, Keesha Riley called and said the very same thing."

"Okay, I'll call them both when we're done talking. And I'm glad you like my hair," Nikki answered, irritated because she knew there was more to come.

"You had a good time with Jeff tonight, honey?"

Nikki nodded. *Come on, Gram, spit it out and get it over with!*

"Well, I'm not totally sure how to begin here," Gram said, smoothing the ends of her robe's tie belt over and over.

After a few seconds of silence on her grandmother's part, Nikki gave a short, uneasy laugh. "Just go ahead and—jump right in, okay, Gram? I know you think we were doing something wrong!"

"Oh, Nikki." She looked up then, straight into Nikki's eyes. "I love you so much. And I don't want to see anything else bad happen to you. And you see—I love Jeff, too," she hurried to add. "I can still picture him, that first summer the Allens moved in next door. He was just learning to walk, and it was the hottest summer I ever remember here. And there was little Jeff, toddling around in the yard in nothing but a diaper, giving your grandfather and me these big, proud smiles every time we stepped outside. And those blue eyes—he does have beautiful eyes, Nikki. But I suspect you've noticed that. And even back then, his eyelashes were way too long to waste on a boy, I always said."

Nikki nodded and tried to be patient. Whatever Gram was trying to get out, it obviously wasn't easy for her to say.

Gram stood up and crossed her arms in front of her. She began pacing back and forth between the dresser and the bed, exactly the way Nikki had done earlier that evening. "So. I guess what I'm afraid of is that two of the people I love most are getting too close, too fast. There. I've said it." She stopped and looked at Nikki, waiting for a response.

Nikki shook her head and put her hands out to either side. "Gram, I don't want to sound dumb here, but I don't get what you mean. We were just kissing—"

Gram's eyes narrowed, and she pursed her lips and thought for a moment. "Okay, Nikki, let me put this in straight language. I've been watching you and Jeff for the past month, and I think you're spending too much time alone together. I think you may be neglecting other interests. And from what I saw tonight, I'm afraid the two of you are getting more physical than you should." She sat back down on the bed, as though saying it all had exhausted her.

"Gram! *What* other interests are we neglecting? And how can you possibly know whether we're getting more 'physical' than we should—we were only *kissing!* I mean, don't you think you're jumping to conclusions here?"

But oddly, all the time she was objecting, it was as though another tape was running in her head. Scenes of her and Jeff, kissing in the Bronco tonight after he'd told her he loved her. Kissing a *lot*. And the almost overwhelming urge she felt to do more, the urge that reminded her so much of times she'd spent with T.J., times that had led to pregnancy and all the grief that followed. But she couldn't say it, couldn't admit it.

Gram waited for a minute before she answered, sitting calmly with her hands in her lap. Nikki had seen her do it before. Gram called it 'defusing' a situation—letting the tension drop before they talked further. While she did, Nikki sat there miserably as more and more embarrassing scenes with Jeff played in her mind.

Finally Gram spoke, and her voice was soft. "I've been wrong before, Nikki, and I may be wrong now. But I don't think so. When I watch you run into Jeff's arms when he arrives, when I hear people say they can never get through to you on the phone because you and Jeff are *always* talking, then I wonder if you have things in the proper perspective."

And you don't even know about the stuff like Jeff skipping Intervarsity so we could talk longer on the phone, Nikki thought guiltily. She hung her head. If Gram had scolded and criticized, it would have been easy to fight back. But her gentle words, her obvious love for Nikki and for Jeff, carried far more weight than scolding.

"Nikki—come sit by me, honey." Gram patted the bed beside her, and Nikki obeyed. Gram circled her with one arm and hugged her gently. "May I tell you a story? From my own memories?"

Nikki nodded.

"Last year you discovered some things about my past that shocked you. But we only gave you the bare facts, none of the details that might help you understand why this situation is worrying me so much. You already know that I made a very bad mistake and got pregnant while your grandfather—then my fiancé—was in Korea, fighting the war. But I never told you how it all started in the first place.

"I certainly never meant to get involved with someone else while he was gone. I loved your grandfather. But I was lonely—U of M was a big place even in those days. At least it seemed big to a scared freshman from tiny little Rosendale. And the other music student, the one you found out about last year, seemed so kind, so concerned about me. There were talks—long talks—and gradually, we started doing things together, going places. I thought at the time that he was the best thing that could've happened to me—it seemed so good to have a friend, you know? But the choices I was making—to spend all my free time with him—were choices that excluded other people and left us alone together most of the time. And eventually, that led to the wrong kind of . . . intimacy."

"But it's not *like* that with Jeff and me, Gram. We're Christians! We don't mean for anything to happen like what you're talking about."

"Nikki, do you think we *did*? I was just lonely and glad to find a friend. But after years of watching young men and women together, I can tell you that it matters little what you *mean* to happen. What matters is that when God made men and women, He built some very strong urges into their bodies, forces designed to bring you together in an intimate way. The Bible talks a lot about keeping our bodies pure; but once you start to spend the majority of your time alone together, and you cut other people and activities out of your life, it gets easier and easier to obey those desires, whether you mean to or not. And no matter what TV and movies tell you, that kind of thing should be reserved for marriage."

"So what are you saying? That you want us to stop seeing each other? Is that what this is all about?" Nikki got to her feet again and resumed her pacing.

"Is that what you think I really want, Nikki?"

"It sounds like it to me!"

"Then let me spell it out plainly. I think very much that Jeff may be the one for you. I've thought that for years, though I don't pretend to know God's will. I don't expect you to stop seeing him at all. What I hope you will do, though, is redefine your relationship. Maybe write some new ground rules."

Gram got to her feet then. "I've said enough for now. Maybe more than enough." She laughed shakily, and Nikki saw how hard this had been for her. "Would you just give it some serious thought, Nikki? Please?" She turned to leave the room, then turned back again. "I remember how easy it is, when you're falling in love with someone, to let them take up even the time you should be spending with God. But that's what you need most when you're trying to decide how to handle a relationship." She kissed Nikki on the forehead and said good night, then shut the door gently behind her.

Nikki felt both guilty and embarrassed when Gram left. She hadn't even admitted to herself yet how confused she felt when she and Jeff spent too much time kissing. On the one hand, she loved it. On the other, uneasiness about it had been building up inside her.

She sat back down on the window seat, drew her knees up, and rested her forehead on them. *I, of all people, should know better. After what happened with T.J., especially. Maybe,* she thought, *I'll never learn to get this right!*

She remembered, with remorse, that only a month ago she had determined to spend regular time with God. Her plan had been to read five psalms and a proverb each day, and to keep a journal of what she'd learned, what she was praying about. Instead, every spare moment had been used up on the phone with Jeff. She opened the drawer of the bedside table and took out the journal. The last entry was September 15.

Nikki held the journal silently for a moment. She sensed deep inside that if she kept going the way she was, she might be headed for more trouble. She certainly didn't want that.

Then again, what if she did—how had Gram put it—*redefine* their relationship? She thought about *not* kissing Jeff, *not* spending hours on the phone with him. After all the time it had taken for them to finally become a real couple, she couldn't imagine ever giving that up.

When the phone rang close to her ear on Saturday morning, Nikki felt around on the bedside table for it without even opening her eyes. "H'lo?" she mumbled, expecting to hear Jeff's voice.

Instead, it was Rachel's. "Nikki! I finally got through to you! I apologize for calling so early, but I'm having a terrible time getting through in the evenings. I thought your grandparents had call waiting!"

Nikki thought of all the times she'd been on the phone with Jeff and ignored the little click that indicated another call coming in. "So, how are you?" she asked, trying to change the subject. She opened one eye and squinted at the clock. 8:00. *And on a Saturday, yet*, she thought, sighing.

"I'm doing all right, thank you. But I really need to talk to you for a minute. Are you awake now?"

Nikki groaned. "I don't think so. Give me a minute, would you?" She sat up in bed, arranging the pillows behind her back, then rubbed sleep from her eyes till she could see the room clearly. Sun was pouring in through the shade she'd forgotten to close. "Okay. What's up?"

"T.J. came by the house yesterday."

Oh, no, Nikki thought. She'd put that issue out of her mind since the discussion with Gram last night, but now she remembered her irritation. "Yeah, Mom, he called me and said you gave him my number. I thought you weren't going to do that! I mean, didn't I ask you not to?"

"Let me explain, okay, honey? When he came by, we were in the middle of the Bible study that meets at the house. I could tell he really wanted to talk to me, so I invited him in and asked him to join us, and he did! There are three other students there from the college, and I think that helped. He actually sat through the whole meeting."

Nikki frowned. The idea of T.J.—Millbrook soccer star, heavy drinker, and the father of her baby—at a Bible study was too outlandish. *What a fake!*

"After the Bible study, the other kids asked him to go out for pizza, so he didn't hang around very long—just long enough to tell me that when the two of you met at the 7-Eleven on Saturday, you made some remark about being pregnant."

Nikki's shoulders sagged and she slid down a bit into the bed. This was even worse than she'd imagined.

"He said that the night you two were—well, were together—he'd been drinking a lot and didn't remember exactly what happened."

Oh, isn't that great? Nikki thought in fury. *I get pregnant and T.J. can't even remember what happened!*

"Then he asked me straight out if you had really been pregnant."

"You didn't *tell* him, did you?" Nikki cried.

"I told him he needed to talk to you directly," Rachel said.

"Listen, T.J. has no business knowing *anything* about me, Mother, and I have to tell you, I was pretty upset that you gave him my phone number." She took a long, slow breath and tried to calm down. "Well, at least you didn't tell him about Evan."

"Nikki, don't fool yourself. He knows. He wasn't totally sure from your comment, whatever it was. But he *had* to know when I wouldn't give him a direct answer."

"Great," Nikki said. "Now it'll be all over Millbrook, and—"

"You know," Rachel cut in, "I didn't get that impression from the way he acted. I don't know exactly how to describe it, Nikki, but I get the feeling that something else is going on here—as though T.J.'s doing some serious thinking."

"Well, I guess there's a first time for everything!" Nikki shot back. "But he can do his serious thinking without me, because I'm not talking to him. You tell him so for me, next time he comes by for a little chat."

There was a long pause. Then Rachel said slowly, "You know, it sounds almost as though we've switched places here."

"What's that supposed to mean?"

"For years, *I* was the sarcastic one—always angry, never able to forgive anybody. But now—" She let the sentence hang, but Nikki felt as though she'd been hit in the stomach.

"Well," Rachel went on at last, "you weren't the only thing T.J. and I talked about, just so you know. The people at Bible study were praying for your father and other people, like we always do, and T.J. wanted to know what was going on and why we pray for them. We talked a little about that, too. What seemed to interest him most was the idea that someone who had hurt other people could be forgiven, not just by God, but by the people involved."

Nikki's mind was spinning. It was more than disturbing to see Rachel able to handle all this so well, especially when Nikki felt like she was drowning in anger. Anger at T.J.—and maybe anger at her father, too. In all her busyness, she hadn't been taking time to pray for her father. *Or maybe*, she thought, *it's more than just being busy.*

❦ *Ten* ❦

AT 10:00, JEFF GAVE A quick knock at the kitchen door and looked inside hesitantly. Gram glanced up from the bacon sizzling in the frying pan and called, "Since when do you have to knock, Jeff Allen?" Gallie gave a repeat of his welcome performance the day before, his tail wagging wildly against Jeff's legs.

Nikki, who was pouring batter into the hot waffle iron, gave a sigh of relief that Gram was trying to make this easier. But she couldn't help noticing that Jeff seemed uneasy, on edge.

Nikki kept one eye on him, trying to reassure him with her smile, and the other on Gram, wondering what she was thinking. *She couldn't have just forgotten last night, that's for sure.*

Grandpa seemed the only one unaware of the tension. Nikki had set the dining room table so they could eat in front of the bay window. As he ate his bacon and waffles, Grandpa commented on the heavy bank of clouds that was moving in across the lake, turning the sky a drab brownish-gray. He polished off two cups of coffee and downed a full glass of orange juice, all the while pointing out the bluejays and chickadees fluttering at the birdfeeder outside.

Nikki was relieved when Jeff finally relaxed enough to join in the conversation. "Nikki and I thought we'd go into Grand Rapids, if that's okay with you. That traveling exhibit—the one about base-ball—is only at the museum for another couple of weeks. And then

I thought we'd grab something to eat at one of the restaurants downtown. Will that be okay with you? Both of you?"

Grandpa gathered his napkin together and laid it beside his plate. "No problem, Jeff. I know Nikki got all her schoolwork done yesterday so she could spend the time with you. Just be careful driving in."

Nikki glanced quickly at Gram, but her face betrayed nothing.

Grandpa went on, "Carole and I went in and saw that exhibit a few weeks ago, and I think you'll enjoy it. I'd kind of like to see it again, but I believe we have a date at the grocery store. Right, sweetheart?"

It wasn't till they were riding in the Bronco that they could really talk.

Jeff questioned Nikki hesitantly. "Is everything okay with you, Nik? I mean, after last night? It was pretty awkward for you, and I apologize for putting you in such a bad spot."

Nikki chose her words carefully, staring out the window at the bare pastures, gray-brown as the clouds, that flew past. "Gram talked to me last night after you left. She was concerned—*is* concerned—that maybe we're getting, well, too—close."

"Yeah?" Jeff's voice was strained, and when Nikki glanced sideways at him, she could see his lips were pressed tightly together, and the telltale red patches were spreading across his cheekbones.

But all he said, after a few awkward seconds, was, "And what do you think, Nik?"

Nikki twisted her fingers together, looking at her rose-colored nails without really seeing them. "I don't know what to say, Jeff." She thought back to some of the verses she'd read in Proverbs that morning, after the conversation with her mother. "Well, maybe that's not quite true. Maybe I do know, and I just don't want to."

Jeff checked the mirrors, signaled a left turn, then passed the car in front of them. "Could you be a little clearer, please? Does this mean your grandmother doesn't want you going out with me anymore?" His voice was tight and flat-sounding, and Nikki quailed inside at the thought of upsetting him.

"No! If you'll just be patient, Jeff, I'll try to explain. This isn't the easiest thing in the world to talk about." She shifted in the seat so they sat farther apart. "Gram loves you just as much as she does me, Jeff, she was clear about that. So it's not like she's criticizing you or anything. But she talked to me some about what happened years ago when she was at U of M. You remember about the letter I found last winter, and—"

Jeff nodded. "I remember."

"Okay, well, she said she and that music student she was involved with got too close because they spent way too much time together. And they let other friendships go. That kind of stuff. And I guess—well, I guess shutting everyone else out of their lives made it easier for them to—to make wrong decisions about how close they got. Physically, I mean."

Jeff blew a long, controlled breath out between pursed lips. Nikki sensed he was as upset as she was, but she couldn't be totally sure, because he had gone distant and very quiet. They were nearing the museum when he turned to face her at a red light.

"Nik, how important is it to you to see this exhibit?"

"Not very," she answered.

"What if I buy you something to drink instead?"

Nikki agreed, and when Jeff parked the red Bronco, they walked a few blocks to the Amway Grand Plaza. There were several restaurants in the building, and Jeff led her to a small, casual one at the back of the hotel which looked out on the Grand River. Brunch smells, mixed with the subdued clink and clatter of dishes, surrounded them. Jeff ordered a café mocha, but when it arrived he only made ridges and lines in the whipped cream with his spoon.

Nikki's own hot chocolate was steaming and frothy, and she sipped it cautiously. Sensing it was important to give Jeff time to express what was on his mind, she cut diagonal lines—one after the other, evenly spaced—into the burgundy paper placemat with her fingernail.

"Nikki," he said at last, "I feel like I'm such a jerk. Your grandparents must think so, too. And that's not the worst part." He broke off and looked out at the river flowing by, watching the water before he went on. "Remember last winter? When I told you about a retreat I'd gone to? About how things happened to me there—spiritually, I mean?"

Nikki nodded, but Jeff went on without looking at her, his eyes still on the swirling, gray water flowing beneath the arched stone bridge outside. "I made some promises at that retreat, Nik. Promises to God and to myself. There was this speaker there who made a lot of sense—a guy not much older than me—and he talked about dating and staying pure and using your time wisely while you're single. And—" Jeff's gaze shifted to her face, and he pointed at himself with the spoon. "And I've broken those promises."

"Jeff!" Nikki cried, suddenly scared at what he might be about to tell her. Then she looked around the restaurant hurriedly and lowered her voice. "What do you mean, you've broken those promises?"

Jeff pushed his cup to the side. Twice he started to talk again, then looked around the restaurant miserably. "I'm sorry. I can't talk about this here, Nikki. I thought I could, but it's not working. Could we just go home and talk where we usually do? Out on the pier?"

The waitress glanced at their nearly-full cups and then looked at them strangely when Jeff asked for the bill. "Is there a problem?" she said.

"Yeah," Jeff said, then saw the look on her face and added hastily, "not with your food or anything, though. We just need to leave."

They rode home in silence, and Jeff didn't even reach for her hand. The clouds were starting to show ragged tears, pulled apart by a brisk southwest wind.

Jeff seemed to relax a little once they were seated at the end of the old pier, listening to the gentle slap of water against the concrete base and the metallic clink of the clips on the pier flagpole. A lone gull cried its way down the lakeshore and disappeared in the distance before he started to talk again.

"I think I've been fooling myself into doing what *I* wanted with this relationship. I kept thinking, man, I've waited so *long* for you, Nikki. And I've been telling myself, we're not doing anything *wrong*. We're not going 'too far,' we're not sleeping together. As far as most people are concerned, we're doing great—a lot better than average, at least."

Nikki raised her eyebrows and waited. She knew how Jeff felt about being average.

"Inside, though, I guess I knew all along I was breaking the promises I made last year. And I wouldn't admit it, even to myself, because then I'd have to change what I was doing. But when your grandmother surprised us in the kitchen, I kind of saw myself through her eyes. That hit me pretty hard, because I feel like I didn't just fail you, I failed your grandparents. I even failed God."

Nikki started to reach her hand out to him, then stopped herself. "Exactly what promises did you make, Jeff?"

He looked down at the table, remembering. "That God would be first. Always. In every single thing in my life. But then, as soon as you and I got together, I stopped asking what *He* wanted."

Fear settled into Nikki's heart, chilling her. "Are you saying that—that you're not sure God wants us to be together?"

Jeff looked up at her, his eyes reassuring. "No, Nik. I'm sorry I wasn't clearer. Guess I was kind of thinking out loud. I've believed for a long time that God wants us to be together. I would never have told you I love you if I didn't know that.

"But we don't know exactly how it'll all work out. You haven't even graduated high school yet, and I've got years of college and grad school ahead of me. And I know you want to finish college and—It just goes on and on, doesn't it? And if we let ourselves get this physical now, where will that put us in four years? Or six?

"I wouldn't let myself think it all through honestly. I just wanted so much to hold you and kiss you—" Jeff's shoulders sagged and he put one hand to his forehead, his thumb and forefinger rubbing the skin back and forth. "And I'm supposed to be the leader in this relationship. Nikki, I think I owe you an apology. No, I *know* I do."

They sat silently for a few minutes. Jeff did what he always did when they talked here—pried pebbles out of the crumbling concrete of the pier with his thumb, then dropped them with a hollow *thunk* into the gray water below their feet. Nikki watched him go through the ritual several times before she spoke.

"It wasn't all you, you know."

He looked up in surprise.

"Nobody forced me to go along with all the physical. I wanted to. Very much. And I'm probably more at fault because—well, because I know better. From experience." Nikki ducked her head, her cheeks burning, glad that Jeff had the good sense to simply sit quietly and wait for her to finish.

"Every time we got close that way, I'd find myself thinking about T.J.—how I blew it with him, and how awful a mistake that was. But I kept pushing the thought away, because I didn't want to face the truth about what we've been doing, either."

She almost went on then, almost told him about T.J.'s call and what her mother had said. But even then, as close as they were, she still couldn't bring herself to share that part. "So I guess you're not the only one who's failed."

Jeff shifted his position a little on the concrete and stared out at the horizon. "The decisions I'm making are starting to affect other people, too, Nikki. You know how I skipped that Intervarsity meeting the other night just so we could talk? My roommate was just about to start coming." He looked up at her, and his eyes were troubled. "But when he saw I didn't go this week, he changed his mind," Jeff said.

Nikki winced. "Yeah, my mother and Keesha are both complaining that they can never get through on the phone anymore. And Keesha's ticked because I don't have time to do things with her. I guess I haven't exactly been the greatest friend lately."

Jeff sat up straight and looked over at her. "Nikki, what would you think if I went back to U of M this afternoon?"

Her heart sank, but she tried not to show it.

Jeff went on. "I think what I'd like to do is take the rest of the weekend to think about all this. And pray about it. I'll probably give Mom and Dad a call, too, and get some advice from them. I don't know about you, but I think I need to get some things straightened out."

Suddenly, with Jeff's support, Nikki knew she wanted more than anything in the world to have their relationship look the way God wanted it to. Still, it was hard to think of Jeff leaving a whole day early. "You couldn't get them straightened out right here, I suppose?" she ventured.

Jeff looked at her and raised his eyebrows. "Nikki, give me a break! When you're right next door, do you really expect me to be able to think about anything but you? I need for us to take the next few days and not see each other, and maybe not even talk on the phone. We could come up with some ideas about how we should act with each other. What do you think?" Jeff asked, his face intense.

Nikki thought for a moment, then nodded. "I want things to be right with us, Jeff. Really right, I mean. I know I blew it before, but—"

Jeff held up one finger to her lips to silence her. "Hey. Don't do that. I mean, don't always go back to what happened last year. You're forgiven, right?"

Nikki nodded, listening carefully.

"Then you're free of what happened before. We can start our relationship clean and fresh, and set up new standards. And *keep* them."

Nikki nodded again, wanting to agree wholeheartedly. But she had seldom felt less free of T.J. She felt as though she was close enough to see the freedom Jeff was speaking of; yet her anger at T.J. was like a chain that kept pulling her back to her old life, forcing her to think of him, again and again.

They walked slowly back toward the beginning of the pier, side by side, not even holding hands for the first time in a long time. It was a relief to get back to small talk, laughing together about what the waitress in Grand Rapids must have thought of them when they left so suddenly, about the museum display they'd missed. As they started up the steps to the house, Nikki's curiosity got the best of her. She stopped and turned to Jeff.

"Hey. I've been just—kind of—well, *wondering* about something you said back there on the pier. That you waited a long time for me. Exactly how long *did* you wait, Jeff Allen?"

Jeff shook his head, a touch of a grin on his lips. "I shouldn't give this kind of information away, I know it. Someday when we're old and gray, you'll still be holding this over my head—"

Nikki put her hands on her hips. "How long, Jeff Allen? Just spit it out. *How long?*"

He looked into her eyes then, and his answer was almost too quiet to hear. "Since about fourth grade."

✤ Eleven ✤

IT WASN'T EASY to watch the red Bronco back out of the driveway an hour later. Nikki watched it head down the street, growing smaller and smaller in the distance, and suddenly the day seemed unbearably bleak and empty. *It's almost like I feel more alive when Jeff's around. I enjoy everything more when I'm with him.* But the thought made her uncomfortable, because she could clearly remember feeling exactly the same way when she'd been dating T.J.

Grandpa broke her chain of thoughts when he opened the kitchen door and came to stand beside her on the top step. "Was that Jeff I just heard leaving?" he asked.

Nikki nodded.

"Is something wrong here, honey?" he asked. His voice was troubled, and she could feel his concern. She wondered if Gram had told him about what had happened in the kitchen last night, or about their conversation which followed.

Nikki took a deep breath and made a choice to turn off the self-pitying thoughts. "No, Grandpa, nothing's wrong. Actually, I guess something's very *right* here." She looked up at him and smiled, and the memory of all the talking she and Jeff had done on the pier gave her confidence. She pushed the hair back from both sides of her face and raised her chin, breathing in the fresh air. "Jeff and I decided we need to make some changes in our relationship. Good changes."

She laid her head against his shoulder for a minute to reassure him. "Don't worry, okay, Grandpa? We'll probably talk to you and Gram about all this as soon as we know exactly what we're doing."

Did you and Jeff have lunch in Grand Rapids?" Gram asked when Nikki went back inside.

Nikki shook her head. "Not really. Just hot chocolate."

Gram wrung out a dish cloth and hung it over the faucet to dry. "Well, you must be starved, then. There's leftover pizza. Or the vegetable soup from last night."

Nikki stood at the open refrigerator and tried to make a choice, but her thoughts kept wandering to Jeff driving away.

"Nikki!" Gram called out at last. "Are you maybe trying to cool off the entire house?" Nikki turned to see her grandmother standing by the sink, hands on her hips, a half-smile on her face.

Nikki smiled back and played along. "Yeah. I thought it was kind of hot in here."

"Right! Just take the pizza already," Gram said. "Eating will take your mind off Jeff for at least a minute."

Grandpa helped himself to some coffee and switched on the radio. "I want to find out how those kids in New Jersey are doing," he said to no one in particular as he settled into a chair at the kitchen table.

Nikki was just about to ask what he meant when the news came on. She listened with growing horror as the announcer reported that one of the three girls who had been shot in a New Jersey middle school the day before had now died.

"Wait a minute! When did *this* happen?" Nikki cried after the reporter finished.

"At the very end of school yesterday," Grandpa answered, stirring his coffee slowly, staring into the brown liquid as though searching for answers. "We didn't hear until the eleven o'clock news last night."

"I never heard a thing about it," she said, tears in her eyes. "Jeff and I had so much to talk about that we didn't even turn on the radio this morning." She listened to the rest of the news story, then stared at the slice of pizza in her hand. She set it back on the plate in front of her and pushed back her chair slowly. "I guess I'm not really hungry after all. I think I'll go up to my room."

"Nikki?" Grandpa stopped her as she reached the doorway to the hall. "Are you sure there's nothing we can do to help? Nothing you want to talk about, as far as Jeff's concerned, I mean?"

For a second Nikki toyed with the idea of asking if there were any passages in the Bible that talked about how you were supposed to act when you were going out with someone, then shook her head. "Thanks, but things are okay, really. Jeff and I just need some time to—to kind of think things through, you know? Make sure we're making the right decisions."

Gram caught her eye and smiled, and Grandpa said, "Okay, honey. And about the school shootings—I wouldn't worry too much about anything like that happening around here."

Nikki looked at him with a question in her eyes. "Even with the threat that was called in?"

He scratched the back of his neck slowly, as though considering her question. "My feeling is that the call was most likely a hoax. Unless we hear something more, I mean."

In her room, Nikki took her Bible and journal off the bedside table and curled up on the window seat. The dark gray clouds finally swept in from the horizon toward the shore like a curtain. As they blotted out the sunlight, Nikki couldn't help but think of the girl in New Jersey who had died in the school shooting.

She wondered how it would feel to stare into the face of a gun, to know the pain of a bullet ripping into you. She tried to figure out what could make a person fire a gun into someone else, and her mind went to the fire and threat at Howellsville. Raindrops hit the windowpane in a burst of sharp spatters, then settled quickly into a steady downpour, water streaming down the glass and distorting the view of the lake beyond.

With effort, Nikki shook off the gloomy thoughts. *I hope Jeff gets back to Ann Arbor before the rain gets there,* she thought. She pictured him driving along in the Bronco and smiled. On the one hand, she was so proud of Jeff, of the way he wanted to please God in every single thing. But she struggled a little at the same time. *Why can't we just be like everybody else?* she thought. *You'd never catch Keesha or Hollis or Noel worrying what God thought about their private dating life. Seems like they just do what everybody else is doing and never give it a second thought.*

On the other hand, Keesha had already gotten pregnant twice, doing what everybody else was doing. Nikki knew she didn't want to model her behavior after Keesha. She thought about Hollis and Noel, about their strong interest in abortion, and wondered if, just maybe, their own dating relationships had gotten out of hand. *Like mine did, with T.J.*

But even thinking of T.J. was a mistake. Just the thought of his name made her blood boil these days. No matter what she did, she couldn't seem to rid herself of the picture of his face, or the sound of his voice on the phone the night before.

Nice time to decide you finally want to find out what really happened, T.J. Now that it's all over and done with, and Evan's growing up in some-body else's family! The memory of their phone conversation made her angrier than ever. *Where were you when I really needed you, anyway? When Evan needed you?* She knew she was being unfair to him, since she'd never told him about Evan, but logic did nothing to stem her anger.

She imagined herself back in Millbrook, running into T.J. and his latest girlfriend. Maybe they'd see each other at the mall, she thought. Or at a soccer game with lots of onlookers standing around. She pictured herself announcing to all of them, particularly to his girlfriend, what a loser T.J. really was. *How would you feel if I did that, Mr. Soccer Star?*

Even better would be to wait until he got married, she thought sud-denly. *Then I could tell his wife what he's really like!* Nikki felt a tremen-dous surge of satisfaction from the very idea of paying him back. At the same time, something deep inside her felt surprised, even ashamed, that the desire for revenge could be so strong. Yet she seemed unable to let go of her want to hurt him.

I need to forget about T.J. and focus on what Jeff and I are trying to build together, she thought. Nikki forced herself to concentrate on the present, and turned back to her Bible. Psalms and Proverbs, where she was trying to have regular devotions, weren't the kind of thing she wanted right now, though. She needed something specific to the situation she and Jeff were facing.

When Nikki had first become a Christian the winter before, Aunt Marta had shown her how to use the concordance in the back of her Bible. She turned to it now, wondering what to look up. Words like "dating" wouldn't be in the Bible, she knew, or "romance." She thought of several other words that might work, then remembered Gram saying, "The Bible talks a lot about keeping our bodies pure," when they'd talked the night before. Under "body," the concordance listed I Corinthians 6:18-20. Since she had never looked at Corinthians before, as far as she could remember, it took a while to find the verses. When she did, she was stunned at how blunt they were.

"Flee from sexual immorality. All other sins a man commits are outside his body, but he who sins sexually sins against his own body. Do you not know that your body is a temple of the Holy Spirit, who is in you, whom you have received from God? You are not your own; you were bought at a price. Therefore honor God with your body."

Nikki frowned. On the one hand, she didn't really think she and Jeff were being "sexually immoral." They'd certainly never slept together, or even come close. On the other hand—

Nikki leaned her forehead against the window the way she often did when she was deep in thought. *On the other hand, I don't exactly feel like a "temple of the Holy Spirit" when all I think about is being with Jeff. It's almost like I belong more to Jeff than I do to God some days.*

She squirmed uncomfortably on the window seat, wishing she hadn't had that last thought. Instead, she looked back at her Bible, hoping to find a way out of this. There was another reference listed by the verses she'd just read: Romans 12:1-2. *At least I know where Romans is,* she thought as she leafed a few pages back in her Bible to find the passage.

"Therefore, I urge you, brothers, in view of God's mercy, to offer your

bodies as living sacrifices"—Nikki wasn't too sure she liked the sound of that—*"holy and pleasing to God—this is your spiritual act of worship. Do not conform any longer to the pattern of this world, but be transformed by the renewing of your mind."*

That part sounded good—about being holy and pleasing to God. She tried to think what that would mean when it came to dating Jeff. She thought back over their recent times together and blushed a little.

It wasn't so much that they'd *done* anything wrong. It was just that, when they were kissing and being close, it made her *want* to do so much more. And deep inside, she sensed she was igniting extremely strong feelings in Jeff, too. Feelings that he was now acting guilty about. No matter how she tried to deny it, she knew that was wrong. *And worst of all, I'm thinking about the whole physical part of our relationship more and more. In fact, being with Jeff is just about all I think about these days.*

"Help me, Lord," she prayed. "I really do want to get this right. I'm just not sure what it means to be holy."

She read through the rest of the chapter, looking for more clues. What she found near the end of the chapter took her in a direction she hadn't expected, however. *"Do not repay anyone evil for evil,"* verse 17 said. The verse seemed to be addressed directly to her, and it grabbed her attention even though it had nothing to do with the relationship between her and Jeff.

Nikki read on. Verse 19 was even worse. *"Do not take revenge, my friends, but leave room for God's wrath, for it is written: 'It is mine to avenge; I will repay,' says the Lord."*

She thought with guilt of her daydreams about T.J. just a few minutes before. "Well," she said aloud, partly to herself and partly to God, "it's fine to talk about not taking revenge. But I don't know anybody who actually lives that way."

She stopped, suddenly realizing that she *did* know someone who lived that way, at least for now. As far as she could tell, Rachel showed no desire for revenge toward Nikki's dad.

Nikki wondered if she could ever be like that, but her anger at T.J. surged again. "Listen, God, T.J. can't just get off scot-free. That wouldn't even be fair!" she cried. The rain had let up a little, and she stared at the drops still hitting the windowpane. They flattened against the glass, skittering sideways in the wind. "And what about *me*? I tried to do what was right and have the baby instead of getting an abortion. And it wasn't easy—You *know* that! But nothing bad happened to T.J.! He didn't have to move away from his home, he didn't lose anything. He just went right on with his life like nothing happened!"

She waited a long time, wishing for an answer, watching the wind whip the water into sharp ridges all across the surface of the lake. If only God would let her know that He understood. That unfairness like T.J.'s couldn't possibly be overlooked, and that maybe—just maybe—a little revenge might be in order.

Instead, the phone rang, and Nikki found the interruption a relief. She went to the hall to get it.

"Hello?"

It felt like an eerie repeat of last night's conversation, only this time Nikki recognized T.J.'s voice instantly.

"Is that you, Nikki?" he asked.

Everything in her wanted to hang up on him again, but the words from Romans 12 kept ringing in her ears. "*Do not repay anyone evil for evil . . .* "

At last she answered him. "This is Nikki."

"Good. Glad I got through to you again. Listen, there's something I really need to talk to you about."

"T.J.," Nikki began, trying hard to control herself, "I don't mean to be rude. I'm sorry I've been hanging up on you. But I made it as plain as I possibly could yesterday: I don't want to talk to you."

"Nikki, *please*. Listen to me. I just want to ask you one question and hear your answer. I have to, don't you see?" His voice sounded different than she'd ever heard it before, almost pleading.

She hesitated, then said, "Get it over with."

"Okay." Nikki heard him take a deep breath before he spoke. "When you said that on Saturday—about pregnancy, I mean—well, were you serious? Or were you just making a crack to get at me?"

That's two questions, T.J., she thought, but didn't say it.

"Nikki, please. Answer me."

"Just a minute, T.J. I need to take the phone where I can talk." She went back to her bedroom and shut the door behind her, then curled up on the bed. Suddenly she felt cold all over, and she pulled the comforter up over her legs. "All right. Yes. When I talked to you on Saturday, I was serious."

There was silence on T.J.'s end then. When he finally spoke again, his voice was hushed. "You mean you really got pregnant that night?"

"Yeah, T.J., I *really* got pregnant." Nikki tried to keep the bitterness out of her voice, but failed.

"But why didn't you ever *tell* me? Why didn't you even *say* anything about it?" he demanded.

"Why didn't you ever even *look* at me again, T.J.?" she countered. "After that night we were together, it was like I became this totally invisible person to you. You wouldn't even say hello in the hall at school! I felt like—like—someone you hired for 20 minutes, then threw away!" Suddenly she was reliving that night, and she couldn't keep back the tears, which made her even angrier. "All you did at Lauren's that night was go back out in the family room and drink with your stupid friends when you were finished with me!" she sobbed. "You were so drunk I had to *walk* home—"

"Nikki," he broke in quietly, "I was so drunk, I don't remember anything that happened that night."

"Oh, right! Now *there's* a likely excuse!" she shot back. "I'll work real hard on believing that one!"

There was a long silence before T.J. answered. "Nikki, I'm not trying to make any excuses. I just want to find out the truth here. Look, I mean, I hate to even say this, but are you sure—I mean, do you know that I was the one who—"

Nikki's rage boiled over. "You listen to me! I never, *ever*, slept with another guy. I know that kind of thing was really in with you and your friends, but it wasn't with me. I *cared* about you, and that's absolutely the only reason I ever let you go that far—"

"But Nikki, you've gotta believe me, I didn't mean for this to happen."

"Well, surprise! Apparently it can happen even when you don't mean for it to!"

They were both quiet then, and Nikki thought of boxers breathing hard in their respective corners of the ring, taking a break.

After another long pause, T.J. spoke again. "Uh, Nikki—this is really awkward. I don't even know how to ask you this, but—"

But Nikki broke in. "You're right, T.J, this *is* really awkward. You said you had one question, but you've asked a whole lot more than one. You got what you wanted—like *always*—and I'm done talking now."

"But there's more we need to say! When can we—"

"Never, T.J. Never!" she said, then hung up before he could reply.

❧ *Twelve* ❧

AFTER THE WAY Jeff and Chad had faced off at Rosie's on Friday night, Nikki wasn't sure what to expect when she walked into school on Monday. She was relieved when Chad didn't show up in Current Events class.

Aside from all the talk about the New Jersey school shooting, and speculation about the threats and vandalism at Howellsville High School, morning classes were routine. It began raining again after third period, so Nikki decided to buy lunch in the cafeteria rather than go out somewhere. She was sitting alone at a table by the windows when Hollis stopped directly in front of her.

"Would you mind if I—I mean, are you waiting for somebody else?" she asked.

Nikki motioned to her to sit down, thinking how odd it was to see Hollis act tentative. "Go right ahead. I'm not expecting anybody else to come."

Hollis slid onto the bench and took a container of cherry yogurt from her bag. She made a long production of peeling back the silver foil top and scraping every bit of pink yogurt off it into the container. Nikki pushed limp, grayish-green string beans back and forth on her tray with a fork, waiting. At last Hollis began spooning yogurt to her mouth, talking at the same time.

"I'm sorry about last week, Nikki. At Burger King, I mean. Noel can be so—so—"

"Rude?"

Hollis's gaze snapped up from the yogurt to meet Nikki's, and they both burst out laughing.

"That's one word for it, nicer than the one I'd use!" After their laughter died away, Hollis added, "I really wanted to talk to you some more. About the abortion thing, I mean. And—" her voice quavered a tiny bit "—about the God thing, too, I guess."

"Well, what stopped you?" Nikki asked.

Hollis shrugged and hesitated, moving her mouth as though savoring the taste of the yogurt. "It's hard to explain, Nikki, without giving away—well, let's just say there are some things Noel doesn't want to discuss these days. Period. And if I try, she gets really upset." She emphasized her words with a wave of her spoon. "I mean *really* upset."

Nikki was dying to ask what she meant, but suddenly, they weren't alone anymore. Chad strolled into the cafeteria, dressed in his usual neatly-pressed jeans and button-down shirt and sweater. She'd seen Chad in every state of mind from romantic to furious, but one thing she knew for sure—she could never predict how he'd act. And she was plenty worried now about his reaction to Jeff's words at Rosie's

I'll just ignore him, she thought, but he made that impossible. He sat down across the table from her, right beside Hollis, then leaned toward her.

"Don't start, Chad," Nikki said, hoping to fend off trouble.

He opened his dark eyes wide, feigning surprise. "Hey, give me a break, Nikki. All I wanted to do was tell you I was sorry about Friday night."

Nikki set her can of Coke down on the table with a little *thump*. "Excuse me?"

Hollis glanced back and forth between Nikki and Chad. "Looks like you two have things to discuss. I'll get out of your way."

"No, stay, Hollis," Nikki said. "You don't need to leave."

But Hollis scraped the last of the yogurt out of the plastic container and ate it, then slung her bag over her shoulder and stood up. "It's okay. I'm finished, anyway. Catch you another time, Nikki."

Once Hollis was gone, Chad gave her the most sincere smile she'd seen from him in months. "I had a couple drinks before we went to Rosie's, and I acted like a jerk. Sorry."

Nikki watched him open a bag of taco-flavored corn chips from the vending machine. After his sudden apology, she was at a total loss on how to respond. "Great lunch," she said finally. "That all you're having?"

"Yeah, well, our gourmet chef left. We're looking for another one, but you know how it is." He raised an eyebrow at her and she couldn't help but smile. His words took her back to last year when they'd been going out. There had been long discussions then about Chad's family, and Nikki's. She knew there wasn't much she could say without bringing up things that hurt him, and she chose her words carefully, picking through them to say the least hurtful thing.

"Is your dad doing okay, Chad? I mean, is he any better than—"

Chad looked up from the corn chips and leveled his gaze at her. His voice seemed eerily matter-of-fact. "My dad's a drunk, remember, Nik? That means he drinks off and on all day, every day. Then he wakes up with a splitting headache and cries and says he's gonna get himself together and never drink again, and all he needs right now is just one little shot to help him with the headache. So he has one little shot; then he has two, then ten, and first thing you know, he's back in his own little world, feeling no pain. Until he wakes up the next morning."

"I thought he went to some treatment place for help last year."

"Oh, yeah. Lasted about two weeks, that one did."

Nikki finally risked putting one of the gray-green beans in her mouth, then made a face at the taste and laid her fork down on the cafeteria tray.

"Does your mother still call?" she asked.

Chad tilted his head back and slid the last of the crumbs from the chip bag into his mouth. "Oh, yeah! Good ol' Mom checks in with us reg-u-lar-ly, just like all the books tell her to do." The cynical look he so often wore suddenly slipped back into place and he aimed his forefinger at her, as though making an important point in a lecture. "And you'll never guess what, Nik. She still 'loves' me, and she still 'wants to be the best long-distance mom she can possibly be.' Which means that, for about three whole minutes every other day, I get her undivided attention on the phone."

His cynical tone turned bitter. "The woman hasn't got a clue. She's off living what she calls her 'new life,' 'doing what's best for her.' And meanwhile," he added, crumpling the chip bag into a tight ball, "guess who's doing the laundry and getting meals and taking care of my old man and . . . " He opened his palm and the ball loosened up, and he held it out as though to show her. "Who cares, anyway? Not me. Not anymore. That's not what I came over here to talk about."

Chad stretched his legs under the table and rubbed her foot with his. "That's some guy you're going out with, Nikki. The preacher, I mean." He winked at her as he waited for her reaction, and Nikki fought the urge to kick him.

"Don't start that again!" she snapped, angry that she'd just spent the last five minutes aching over his pain. "I don't know why you always have to make fun of Jeff. Maybe words are the only way you know to fight back." She felt mean even as she said it. "You sure didn't do a very good job of standing up to him at Rosie's."

She anticipated an angry response, but once again Chad surprised her. He lowered his head and folded his hands in front of him on the table. "You're right, ma'am, you're absolutely right," he said in a quavery voice, and Nikki remembered how he used to make her laugh by the hour when they were dating, imitating voice after voice of movie stars and politicians. He looked into her eyes now, totally straight-faced. "It's my extraordinarily low self-esteem talking, according to the counselor. And I know someday I'll have to deal with it. I know that's true."

"Your 'extraordinarily low self-esteem'? *Right!*" She couldn't help laughing, even though he drove her crazy, and he laughed with her. For a moment it was as though they were still friends, friends who could discuss nearly anything, just as they had been the year before.

It was a dizzying change of direction, but conversations with Chad were always that way.

"Well," Nikki said when their laughter stopped, "just knock it off about Jeff, would you? It really freaks me out when you make fun of him that way."

Chad stared at her for a second, then caught her off guard yet again. In his eyes she saw sudden pain that made her catch her breath. "Don't worry, Nik," he said quietly, "I won't be bugging you much longer."

The bell rang, signaling the end of lunch, but something in the tone of his voice made her stomach knot. She couldn't just walk away. "Chad—" she began, but he shook his head and held up a hand as though to stop her.

"But Chad! I have to know—are you okay?" she persisted.

He shrugged, and she thought he would dismiss her question. Instead, he answered her seriously. "Maybe—sometime when the Jeff man's not around and you have a little spare time—maybe we could talk some more, huh?"

Nikki looked at him in surprise. *Chad?* Wanting to talk? His next words surprised her even more.

"You were about the only one I could ever talk to around here, Nikki."

"Chad," she said as gently as she could, suddenly afraid of where this could lead, "you need to know I'm really serious about Jeff."

"Oh, get over it, would you, Nik?" he said, his voice suddenly angry again. "I don't want to go out with you anymore—I got beyond that months ago and there've been plenty of other girls since! Didn't you ever hear of just being friends?"

She watched him get to his feet and change back into the old Chad, almost as though he slipped on an attitude the way he would his coat. For a second he eyed her cafeteria tray and she thought he might offer to take it for her. Instead, he tossed his crumpled chip bag onto it, then turned and left.

The house was quiet that evening and Nikki was glad. *Maybe I can finally do some serious thinking about this thing with Jeff*, she thought. They had agreed that they wouldn't talk on the phone until the middle of the week, so each of them could take time alone to pray and read Bible passages to get ideas about where they should go with their relationship.

"After we do that," Jeff had said, "we'll compare notes, okay?"

It all sounded so great when Jeff talked about it. When Nikki tried to actually work on it by herself, though, she grew more and more frustrated.

"Honor God with your body," Nikki read again that night in her room, curled up on the window seat with the curtains drawn, the cozy drumming of the rain against the windowpane once again providing a backdrop. *And that's what I want to do, really, God*, she thought. *Honor You. So what does that mean? How do Jeff and I actually do that?*

She opened her journal to the blank pages at the back and began a list. No sex till marriage. That one was a no-brainer, totally obvious from the Bible. She stared at the one item on her list, stuck.

So does this mean we shouldn't kiss? she wondered. *Or hug? What about holding hands?*

Suddenly another thought came into her mind. *And what about a person who's already had a baby out of wedlock, trying to act like she's a virgin?*

Nikki had no idea where the thought had come from, but it made what she was trying to do look suddenly absurd. She laid her pen in the crease of the journal and closed her eyes, trying to block out the voice.

You can't change what you did. Why try to act like it never happened?

Nikki put both hands against her ears, then realized how silly that was. She opened her eyes, blinking back tears. "I won't listen to this!" she said out loud to the empty room. "I asked God to forgive me, and I believe He did. I *know* He did! And I'm going to live the right way now, as soon as I can figure out what that means."

The voice seemed to disappear once she stood up to it, and she breathed a sigh of relief. She picked up her journal again. At the top of the page, above her one-item list, she wrote:

I blew it, I know that. But God forgave me. So I'm starting over, and I'm going to act like I am *pure, like I have standards I want to keep. I won't let what happened before mess me up.* She printed in the date and time, too, to make it seem more definite.

She read the words over and over and began feeling stronger, more determined than ever. But while it was easy to talk about having standards in general, it was still hard to figure out exactly what they should be.

Nikki went back and reread the passages in Romans and I Corinthians again, slowly and carefully. But oddly enough, the same thing happened as had the night before. One phrase kept repeating itself inside her head, filling her mind. *Do not take revenge. Do not take revenge.*

Lord, I'm trying to do something important for Jeff and me here! This is a good thing. I know You want us to do this, and I'm asking for help! she prayed silently.

But instead of help, all she heard was the same phrase over and over, and T.J.'s face came to mind.

Finally she burst out, "Okay, okay, I admit there's a problem here with T.J. But right now, that's not what I'm working on!"

Instantly, she sensed a reply—not with her ears, but with her heart—that said, "But it is what *I'm* working on."

At the end of the evening, Nikki sat frowning at a page that was still nearly blank.

She felt as if she'd hit a brick wall.

❦ *Thirteen* ❧

TUESDAY MORNING THE BUZZ around school was that metal detectors were to be installed by the end of the week. "Oh, man," Keesha groaned, "can you imagine the traffic jam that's gonna make?"

"Guess you'll have to get here earlier!" Nikki teased, then added, "Okay, okay—I didn't mean it!" when Keesha glared at her.

In Current Events class, the issue of abortion came up, just as Noel had predicted, though it didn't seem to be on Ms. Mendoza's agenda for the day. Noel mentioned a news item she'd seen on Monday's *NBC Nightly News*, about a case that had made sensational headlines just a couple of years before.

"Remember those two teenagers who killed their baby and threw it away in a motel dumpster?" she asked. Groans sounded from around the classroom. "Well, the news said they're getting out of jail after two years. At least one of them is. The other one only has to serve another six months or so, and then they do some community service and they're home free! I don't think that's right."

Voices burst out all over the room, but as always when she sensed a hot debate brewing, Ms. Mendoza reviewed what she called her "ground rules."

"Those of you who have done time in my classes know how I run discussions. There are ground rules I will not let you break, remember? And the most important one is that you must respect each other. You can express any honest opinion you want to, but you *may not* put other people down. Clear?"

There were nods from all over the room—some grudging, some enthusiastic, Nikki noted. But then, she wondered, what else could anyone do? Nobody in his right mind disagreed with Ms. Mendoza, at least not to her face. She could be pretty awesome when she got upset.

"All right, that's settled. I can see you're all anxious to get in on this one, so I'll put aside the topic I had planned for today." Ms. Mendoza glanced around the room. "When you're ready to talk, stand up, speak up, and then—if I may be so blunt—shut up. Keep in mind that everybody wants the chance to talk, so this is not a time for long harangues."

"Long *what?*" put in Jerry from somewhere behind Nikki.

"*Harangues*, Jerry. Unnecessarily long speeches meant to try to convince . . . Never mind. We need to get going here. Who's first?"

Noel was on her feet before anyone else had a chance, her long, glossy black hair a stark contrast to her bright yellow shirt. "If those two had taken care of the problem the right way, none of this ever would have happened."

"What problem, Noel?" Ms. Mendoza asked. "You'll have to be more specific."

"The pregnancy, of course. It should have been terminated back at the very beginning. Then two people would never have gone to jail, saving taxpayers a huge amount of money. And a baby would never have had to die."

"A baby would still have died!" Nikki burst out before she even realized she was going to speak. She was immediately called down by Ms. Mendoza.

"You can be next, Nicole, but you cannot interrupt." The teacher sighed and looked disgusted. "Didn't I just make this perfectly clear?" She glanced around the classroom with her eyebrows arched as though in question, then sighed again. "Clear as mud, apparently. All right, Noel, go on."

Nikki looked down at her desk, her face burning.

"Way to go, Sheridan!" Chad hissed from behind her. He reached forward and pulled on her leg. "Here. Let me help you get your foot out of your mouth."

"Shut up, Chad!" Nikki hissed back, then cowered when Ms. Mendoza whirled around and glared at her.

When the commotion died down, Noel shrugged one shoulder and said, "That's really all I had to say. Some things are just common sense." She sat back down, pulling her hair to the front over one shoulder so she wouldn't sit on it.

Everyone looked at Nikki, who slid out of her chair hesitantly and got to her feet.

"Sorry I interrupted, but I believe that abortion is killing a living human being, whether you do it at one month or at nine months." Nikki twisted her hands nervously and swallowed hard before she went on. "I know there's a lot of discussion about when life begins, about how late in a pregnancy you can 'terminate' and still not be killing a person. I'm not a scientist or a doctor or anything, so maybe my opinion doesn't matter all that much. But I say that since no one really seems to know for sure when it's a baby and when it isn't, it's crazy to kill it. I mean, I don't know how you could decide that it's okay on one day to kill it, but not the next." Nikki stopped and looked at the others in the room, who gazed back impassively.

I wish I knew how to say something significant, something that would really make a difference. She tried to press her point.

"See, this friend of mine, whose father is a doctor, told me that they're saving babies at younger and younger ages now. He says that just a few years ago, a baby born at, like, six months or so would have died for sure. But now they know how to take care of it and help it and keep it alive. Maybe in the next 10 or 20 years, we'll learn how to keep babies alive no matter how young they're born. And if that's the case, then I think we should realize that killing them is never an option. So I—well, I guess that's all I have to say." Nikki sat down abruptly and felt her cheeks begin to flush.

Noel made a little *hmmm* sound even before Nikki got all the way back into her seat, then slid out of her chair. "I guess I *do* have more to say, now that I think of it." She not only got to her feet, she actually moved to the front of the classroom and looked into the eyes of her classmates. Nikki couldn't help but envy the way Noel's intensity seemed to grab and hold everyone's attention.

"Abortion is a basic right women *have* to have," Noel began. "All this talk about the fetus being a human being is simply an attempt to play on women's emotions. It's the religious right and other ultra-conservatives trying to control by inspiring guilt. If you've ever seen pictures of a fetus, you know that this is *potential* life, not the kind of life you and I have. This is not the kind of life that can survive on its own."

Wait a minute! Nikki wanted to shout. *I have seen a fetus, not just a picture of one, and it's a lot more than potential life. And none of us can survive on our own, not ultimately.* But Noel was still talking, and Nikki didn't dare interrupt again.

"If you argue from the premise that all *potential* life must be protected, then every acorn you ever saw would have to be protected. Every seed of *any* kind. And you could forget having eggs for breakfast, because eggs are *potential* life." Laughter broke out around the classroom. "And it'd have to be protected." Noel made her point, then strode back to her seat and sat down.

"But we're talking about *human* life. And human life is *different!*" Nikki could hardly keep the words inside until she could jump to her feet. She spread her arms to the class. "Don't you see she's making this whole discussion look ridiculous by what she's saying? And that's her *point!* Talking about acorns and—and—*chicken* eggs—that has nothing to do with the real issue, because human life is *different!*"

"How is it different?" Noel put in, sounding bored. "Life is life."

From the seat behind Nikki, Chad spoke. "It's different now that Nikki's got religion, that's how."

Laughs sounded from around the room again. Nikki turned and looked at him, hurt. After lunch the day before, she had thought—had hoped, at least—that they were on their way back to becoming friends again.

Ms. Mendoza raised her eyebrows and folded her arms across

her chest. "Order seems to be breaking down here." She glared at Chad and Noel.

At least she's an equal opportunity glarer, Nikki thought, determined not to have Ms. Mendoza's glare turned back on her another time today.

"Now, if we could please get this discussion back on track . . . Noel, you may continue, but keep it brief. And keep to the subject at hand."

"This *is* the subject, Ms. Mendoza," Noel said politely. "If you take a person's beliefs to their logical conclusion, you can often uncover how erroneous they are."

"Speak English!" Jerry Simoncelli called from the back of the room.

"Get a dictionary," Noel snapped back, and Ms. Mendoza turned her gaze in Jerry's direction, quieting him with one look from those black eyes.

Noel continued as calmly as though she'd never been interrupted. "So I think it's really important for us to look at just how far we want to take this argument of potential life. It can lead us to places we don't want to go. We could find ourselves spending billions of dollars to protect all kinds of things that don't need protecting." She sat down, looking pleased with herself.

Ms. Mendoza nodded in Nikki's direction, as though inviting further comments.

It was almost painful to make herself say anything after what had happened, but Nikki felt she had to point out one thing. "I'll just say that Noel's whole argument rests on the *potential life* thing, but I don't think we're talking about *potential* life. I think we're talking about life, period. When an organism grows, it's living. And if you study what happens with a fetus even in the first few hours, you'll see tremendous growth."

Jordan Wright made one of his pronouncements at that point. "Then you're saying all life on earth should be protected."

"No, Jordan, that's *not* what I'm saying, so stop putting words in my mouth. I'm saying all *human* life should be protected."

"Then you're putting human life in some special category, apart from everything else on earth. You can't do that, because if we all evolved from the same source, one life can't be more important than another." Jordan waited for her reply, one eyebrow raised.

Nikki sighed. She hadn't wanted to go in this direction, because she knew how they would laugh at her, but she could see no other choice. "I believe human life is special because we're made in God's image. We're different from other life on the planet. We have the capacity to know God, and He says not to kill."

Chad laughed out loud, and before Ms. Mendoza could silence him, he said, "And she *always* goes to Sunday School, boys and girls."

Jordan, however, piped up immediately. "I don't think we ought to get into religion here. Isn't that against the rules or something?"

Ms. Mendoza pursed her lips and looked uncomfortable for a few seconds. "I don't think we've crossed any boundaries, but perhaps we should take the discussion in a different direction." She scanned the classroom. "I'm assuming the rest of you have some opinions on abortion."

Allie Herndon got to her feet beside her desk. "I don't really understand why we have to talk about this. The government already decided, didn't it? I mean, abortion's been legal since way before I was born. So if it's legal, why do we have to keep on discussing it?" She sat down, as though she had settled the argument once and for all.

Then Hollis surprised everyone by speaking in a near-whisper from where she sat. "Slavery was legal, but that didn't make it right," she said, glancing warily at Noel.

"Good point, Hollis," Ms. Mendoza said, "but please stand up when you speak. We need to think about that. Is the government always right? And how should we react when we believe the government is wrong? But if we followed that topic up, it would take us into an entirely different subject—civil disobedience. So for today, let's not go farther afield. Back to abortion, and to this case that NBC reported on. Anybody else want to speak up?"

Noel got back up, glaring at Hollis. "Maybe we need to stop worrying so much about trying to figure out when life begins and start figuring out how to take care of the life that's already *here*, you know?" She looked around the room and spread her hands wide as though to invite them all to think with her. "I heard once that something like 30,000 kids die of hunger every day, somewhere around the world. And of the ones that *do* live, look at *how* they live—starving to death a little bit at a time, or dying by inches of some disease that could be prevented if they had even one decent meal a day, and vitamins and clean water." She shook her head in disgust. "It's insane to keep filling up the world with more and more kids who won't get taken care of. And when parents don't want a baby, they're much more apt to get angry and abuse it. That's why we see such an incredible rise in child abuse and—"

"That's not totally substantiated and you know it," Hollis put in, her voice quavering a little. Noel stopped and stared at her. "Well, it's not! When we did all that research for Child Development—remember that project we did last year?—we found out that some of the evidence actually points the other way."

Noel looked annoyed, and her voice sounded tight, as though she was daring Hollis to go on. "*What* other way, Hollis?"

"Remember that one columnist that said that child abuse has actually risen since *Roe vs. Wade* passed? And his theory was that since our country now allows people to get rid of—well, to terminate pregnancies—we don't value life as much anymore. And he thought that maybe that's actually *causing* the rise in child abuse."

Noel shook her head in exasperation. "Hollis! Which side are you on, anyway?"

Hollis looked confused for a moment. "I don't know anymore. Maybe I'm not on any side. Maybe I just want to look at the facts."

Nikki had been fuming inside as she listened, trying desperately to think of something she could say which would clinch the argument, prove that abortion was wrong. But when Hollis said that, Nikki had a sharp, clear stab of memory of herself a year ago, facing this issue for the first time. She, too, had been looking for the "facts," the truth of the issue, the way Hollis seemed to be.

Hollis covered her confusion quickly and reverted back to her usual confident attitude. But Nikki had seen enough to know that there was a struggle going on inside.

Noel was speaking again, and she was angry, Nikki could tell. "Fine, Hollis. You want the facts? Then be quiet for a minute, would you?" She turned back to the rest of the room. "I've basically forgotten what I wanted to say, thanks to the interruption. All I know is, we've got to take care of the people who are already here. And to do that, we might have to sacrifice some of the ones who aren't here yet. And another thing. The guy has to get involved here. Whether the woman decides to abort or not is up to her, because it's her body. And whichever way she chooses, she should have the support of the father."

Allie rolled her eyes. "Let me tell you, if I ever told my boyfriend I was pregnant, 'support' is not the word for what I'd get!" The class laughed with her, but the interruption seemed to only make Noel more intense.

Ms. Mendoza was trying to quell the new interruption, but Noel spoke right over her. "That's exactly what I mean! Look at Allie's reaction, and you'll know why women—especially women our age—*have* to have the right to abort. Men don't support you. They make it impossible to tell them what's going on because of their reactions, then they make life unbearable for you."

"Get off your high horse, Noel!" Chad said, and Nikki was shocked to hear the fury in his voice. She turned around to see him on his feet, his face flushed.

"Chad!" Ms. Mendoza said sharply. "You're interrupting. I expect you to quit, immediately."

Chad gave a snort of derision. "Oh yeah? You're telling me I have to listen to her lump us all together this way?" He turned and spoke directly to Noel, the flush on his cheeks deepening. "You don't know every guy in the world, obviously. We have a say in this, too. Women don't get pregnant alone, in case you haven't noticed that yet."

Noel's voice was cold as ice, her eyes narrowed to slits. "Oh, I've noticed, Chad. I've noticed."

By this time, Ms. Mendoza was at Chad's side. "Chad, you need to sit down, now," she said so quietly that only Chad and Nikki could hear.

"And if I don't want to?"

"Then you can leave."

Chad shrugged, acting nonchalant, but Nikki knew him well enough to know he was only a hair's breadth from exploding. "Fine. I was going anyway."

❧ *Fourteen* ❧

NIKKI'S HEAD WAS SPINNING by the time she left Current Events class. She felt as though she'd just had a glimpse into something very private between Chad and Noel, but didn't have a clue what it was.

She wondered briefly what could be making Chad do these sudden about-faces, from humor to fury to depression. A chill ran down her spine at the memory of his words in the lunchroom: *I won't be bugging you much longer.* The words had a faintly ominous ring to them. But who could ever tell when Chad was serious?

Nikki parked the Mazda in the driveway of the blue clapboard house and went inside, squatting down to hug and pat Gallie, who met her with his usual ecstatic display of affection. He wriggled all over as she smoothed his golden fur, and managed to get in a few wet licks even though Nikki tried to shield her face.

But all of those thoughts evaporated when she found a note on the counter that Jeff had called and would call back later.

I thought we weren't going to talk till midweek! she thought, grinning. It was obvious Jeff couldn't hold out that long, which made Nikki feel a lot better. Ever since he'd left, she had been feeling guilty about her nearly irresistible urge to pick up the phone and dial his number, then make up some excuse. *But now all I have to do is wait for him to call me!*

When he did call, however, the situation wasn't what she'd expected.

"Nikki, I know I said we wouldn't talk till later, but I couldn't wait to tell you this stuff!" Jeff's excitement was bubbling over and his words came fast. "I've been talking to the guy who leads our Intervarsity group here, and he gave me some great sections in the Bible to read and pray about. And I think I've got some ideas worked out—about our relationship, I mean. Wait till you hear them! But first, tell me what you've come up with so far."

Nikki's grandparents were gone, so she sank down on the love seat in the living room to talk. "Well," she began hesitantly, "I didn't get very far yet, Jeff—"

"You didn't? Why not?"

"Well, it's only been a few days, and I just—I—" Nikki fumbled for words. It was the whole situation with T.J. that was getting in her way, she knew. But it wasn't something she could ever discuss with Jeff. *The last thing I'm going to do is tell him about that*, she thought.

"But I thought we were both committed to doing this. I thought it was as important to you as it is to me," Jeff said. His voice sounded flat, as though all his enthusiasm had drained away.

"Oh, it was—it *is!*" Nikki answered. "It's just that—other things kind of keep getting in the way." She realized as soon as she said it how unconvincing the words sounded, and she tried to salvage the situation. "So why don't you go ahead and tell me what you came up with, Jeff? I really want to hear." There was a *click* on the line indicating another incoming call, but Nikki ignored it.

Jeff hesitated, then said, "I don't think I ought to do that. See, Nik, if I just tell you what *I* think and you haven't decided for yourself what guidelines God wants us to have—then it's like you're just going along with what I want, you know? Almost like I'm telling you what to do."

"But Jeff—"

"Nik, I'm serious about this. It has to be something we do together or not at all."

Nikki tried hard to concentrate over the *click* which kept sounding on the line.

"We *will* do it together, Jeff. I'm just having some—some trouble getting started."

"What happened?" he asked. "I thought we agreed to put aside everything we could for the next few days and just work on this. I'm really serious about this." She wasn't sure if it was the disappointment in his voice or the irritation she was feeling at him that made her eyes fill with tears. All she knew was that this was turning into a mess.

"Look, Jeff, I'm *sorry*, I am. You just don't understand what's been going on—"

"Maybe I can help. What's happening?"

Nikki swallowed hard. How could she explain without bringing T.J. into this? How else could she describe what happened each time she tried to pray about her relationship with Jeff? On top of everything else, the *click* sounded again on the phone and she began to grow uneasy about Gram and Grandpa. What if something was wrong and they needed her?

Before she thought of the effect her words would have on Jeff, she said, "Could you hang on a second, Jeff? I need to find out who's on the other line, then I'll be right back."

When she switched lines, she was startled to hear Rachel's voice.

"Mother? Hi! Listen, I'm on—"

"Oh, Nikki! I'm so glad I got through to you! I've done the stupidest thing, and I'm just hoping and praying that Mom and Dad can help me out. Are they there?" Rachel's voice hovered somewhere between laughing and crying, but definitely upset.

"No, they're out shopping or something. What's wrong?"

"I had a faculty meeting that went overtime, so I was rushing to get to class and the heel broke on my shoes—you know those blue heels I wear with the navy suit? I was halfway down the stairs and when it broke, I *fell* the rest of the way. I've been at the emergency room most of the afternoon."

"Well, don't stop there!" Nikki cried, totally forgetting that Jeff was waiting on the other line. "Are you *hurt?* Did you *break* something?"

"No, but the doctor said I'll probably wish I had before this is all over. He says a clean break would have healed easier than a sprain this bad." Rachel's voice was closer to tears now. "I'm sorry, honey. I'm just in so much pain it's hard to think. And they gave me all kinds of pain medicine that's starting to knock me out."

"Mother!" Nikki said, exasperated. "Tell me what you *sprained!*"

"Oh, I didn't say that? It's my right ankle—well, at least it *used* to be my ankle." She gave a little laugh, but her voice was starting to fade. "It doesn't look much like an ankle right now. It looks more like a football, actually—about the same color, same size."

"What will you do? Is somebody there with you?" Nikki asked. "How are you going to get around, and cook and stuff?"

"That's why I called, Nikki. I know it's a lot to ask, but I'm hoping that Mom could take a few days off and come down to help. One of the ladies from my Bible study is here with me right now, but she can't stay. She works third shift, so she'll have to leave before 11:00. The doctor says if I can just stay off this ankle completely for the first three days or so, it'll heal much quicker. After that, he'll give me crutches and I can get around on them. But right now, I have to keep it elevated."

"Gram and I will both come!"

"Nikki, you can't take off school that long—"

"Sure I can! I know Grandpa can't come right away because he's got an article that's due this weekend, and Gram can't drive all that way by herself." Thoughts of school and homework swirled around in Nikki's mind, but she pushed them away. "We can come right away, as soon as they get home. I have almost all my books from school here with me because they gave us a ton of homework today. I'll just bring them with me, and then call the school tomorrow and have them fax my assignments. I'll start packing now, and if we can leave soon, I won't have to drive the whole way in the dark."

"Oh, honey," Rachel said, "I appreciate this so much. The people from my Bible study will help as much as they can, but they all have families and jobs of their own. Now listen, you be careful driving down here, you hear me? It seems like there was something else I wanted to tell you, but I can't remember right now . . . " Her voice had been growing steadily fainter, and by the time she finished, Nikki could hardly make out her words.

"Mom? I can hear the medicine taking effect. Are you somewhere safe where you can just go to sleep?"

"Mmm-hmm. I'm in bed. But there was something that I needed to tell you . . . "

"Mom, please, don't worry about it right now, okay? I'll be there as soon as I can. Just go to sleep." She pushed the TALK button to disconnect.

It was then that Nikki realized two things.

First, she remembered that Jeff was waiting on the other line. She hurriedly switched back, but he was gone.

Oh, no! she thought. *He'll think I didn't even care enough to finish our conversation.* She punched in his number quickly, but the line was busy.

Second, she remembered T.J. If she went back to Millbrook, there would be no way to avoid him.

Her thoughts galloped wildly. *I could call Mother back. I could say the school won't let me miss this much time. I could say I'm sick.* She stopped and shook her head to clear it. It was amazing, the lies her mind could come up with when she felt cornered, even though she had made the decision to never lie again, now that she was a Christian.

Nikki's shoulders sagged as she realized what she was getting herself into.

If this keeps up, it won't be a lie to say I'm sick!

Fifteen

BY THE TIME Nikki's grandparents returned from shopping, Nikki was almost packed. She'd spent 15 minutes putting jeans and shirts and underthings in the biggest of the new suitcases she'd received for her birthday a month earlier.

Even under these circumstances, there was pleasure in touching the soft, buttery blue leather and packing her things neatly inside. Gallie lay in the bedroom doorway looking worried, the way he always did when anyone he loved got out a suitcase.

"Don't worry, boy," she tried to reassure him. "I'll be back before you know it."

He whined in answer, and laid his golden snout flat on his outstretched front legs, never taking his eyes off her. She stepped over him to go and get her things out of the bathroom, and heard her grandparents downstairs.

"Gram? Grandpa?" she called. "Could you come up here for a minute?" She didn't want to lose any time if she could help it, not even enough to run downstairs and explain.

Her grandparents came upstairs, and Nikki explained the situation while she tucked her toothbrush and shampoo and deodorant into her makeup bag.

"Oh, my goodness, I've got to call Rachel right now," Gram said, reaching for the phone. Nikki stopped her, explaining how drugged her mother had sounded.

"She was in a *lot* of pain, Gram. I think the kindest thing to do would be to let her sleep as long as she can, really I do."

"Give me just a few minutes to pack my things, then," Carole Nobles said. She and Grandpa talked out the details as Gram began pulling clothes off hangers and folding them into her suitcase.

"I can drive down as soon as I get this article in," Grandpa said. "Maybe I should call the editor and explain I have to be late—"

Gram straightened up. "Roger! They've already given you two extensions on the deadline. You stay here and finish. Nikki and I can handle this."

"I should be able to get there on Saturday," he said, and Gram gave him a reassuring hug.

"That'll be fine, I'm sure it will."

Grandpa nodded and started carrying Nikki's things downstairs to the car, while Nikki helped Gram finish packing. Before another half hour was up, they were in the Mazda fastening their seatbelts.

"Don't forget your grandmother hasn't eaten anything yet," Grandpa called as Nikki backed out of the driveway.

"We'll stop at McDonald's!" Nikki yelled back, grinning at the face he made.

Because of the aftereffects of the stroke, Gram was not allowed to drive after dark, so Nikki had to drive the entire distance. But having Gram along as company helped. And in all the busyness of getting packed, Nikki managed to put T.J. out of her mind for the time being.

As soon as they got onto the highway, Nikki had to repeat the entire conversation with her mother again for Gram.

"Explain to me again how she sprained it, Nikki."

Nikki recounted the part about Rachel's broken high heel.

"And you said somebody's with her right now, right?"

Nikki reassured her of that, and Gram finally seemed to relax a little. Nikki glanced across the front seat at her profile in the fading light and smiled. She had never seen Gram act like a worried mother about Rachel before, and there was something endearing about it. At the same time, she felt the now familiar pain inside, the pain of missing her own son, Evan. "I guess nobody ever gets so old that their mother doesn't worry about them, right, Gram?"

Gram reached across the seat and patted Nikki's knee. "Never. And when you're not being worried about, you're being prayed for and thought about and loved." She turned and looked at Nikki. "You're finally starting to experience that with your mother, aren't you, honey?"

Nikki nodded. "For all those years, I thought she didn't care about me much at all. I didn't think she ever would. But once she got things straightened out with the Lord—what a difference! I mean, we still have a million things to work out, but—I guess I finally do feel like I have a mom, for the first time in my life." She switched on her headlights, then shrugged one shoulder. "So go figure—now I have a mother, and no father."

"I suspect that's the way it feels, honey, though I can't say I understand. But you do still have a father."

"Right! If you call this having a father." She thought back to their last conversation just a little over a month ago. David Sheridan had driven to Rosendale from Millbrook, not long after he left Rachel and began living openly with another woman. Nikki had been full of emotions—anger and confusion and hurt. But most of all, she'd had hope that their meeting might result in some change in her father.

It had become apparent, however, after just a few minutes together walking on the beach, that David had come only to seek acceptance for what he was doing. He'd angrily pushed away all the pain Nikki showed, refusing to acknowledge that he was the cause. He had insisted that she accept his new lifestyle, and left in a fury when she wouldn't.

"You never know what God will do, Nikki," Gram said. "Look how He worked in your mother's life. Did you ever, in your wildest dreams, think He would change her this way?"

Nikki considered that. "I have to admit that I didn't."

"Well, *I* did!" Gram said.

Nikki glanced at her, startled. "You did? After all those years of praying for her when nothing happened?" She sighed, then added, "But then, you know how to pray. You've been at it for years and years, so I guess it would work for you."

Gram turned halfway in her seat. "Nicole! You mean to say we haven't taught you any better than that?"

"What do you mean?" Nikki asked, surprised.

"I don't think prayer depends on how long you've been 'at it' or how much you know. And it doesn't 'work,' like some magic incantation. *God's* the One who does the work. He's the One who puts the desire to pray for certain things in your heart in the first place. And *He's* the One who *works!* And when you're absolutely sure of God, you can afford to keep praying for someone for however long it takes, because you know He can be trusted to do what's best."

"Whoa! I guess I said the wrong thing back there," Nikki said, feeling a little sheepish. "But I don't have any idea how to pray for Dad right now."

Gram sighed. "I pray a lot of Bible prayers for him. Have you ever looked at the prayers Paul prayed for the people he cared about? But I also pray that he'll find what his heart is really looking for. And you can bet that doesn't mean Celine or Celia or whatever her name is! He could 'fall in love' with a hundred women, but not one of them will ever fill up that emptiness inside him, not for good. Only God can do that. And that's what we need to pray most of all. I'm just sorry you have to get hurt as a result of his search."

"Seems like that's going on everywhere, nowadays—grownups doing their searching at the expense of their kids—" She broke off suddenly and shifted in her seat so that she could look out her side window. "You know what, Nikki? I'm sorry to slow us down, but I really am getting hungry. Maybe even hungry enough for McDonald's."

Nikki turned off at the next exit and went through the drive-up of a fast food restaurant. She had to laugh when even Gram, who detested fast food, admitted how much she was enjoying her fish sandwich.

"My mother used to always say, 'Hunger is the best sauce,' and I guess she must've been right. Thanks for stopping, honey."

It was nearly 11:00 by the time they pulled into the driveway of Rachel's house in Ohio. A small lady, gray-haired, whom Nikki had never met before, answered the door. She smiled broadly when she recognized Nikki.

"You're Nicole!" she said. "I can tell from the pictures Rachel has around the house. And you must be Rachel's mother," she said to Gram. "Rachel was so glad you were coming. I'm Lilly Barnes, from the Bible study group that meets here." She motioned them both inside. "If there was any way I could stay the night, I would. But I've got to be at work in just under an hour."

"Where's my mother?" Nikki asked. "In bed?"

Lilly motioned down the hall. "Actually, she's sleeping in a recliner because the doctor said that was the best way to keep her ankle elevated. Some of the others from the Bible study came by when they heard, and we moved the recliner into her room. You can come and see her, but she's out like a light. The doctor gave her extra pain medicine because he said this first night would be the worst."

Nikki and Gram made their way down the hall to where Rachel's bedroom door stood ajar. Rachel was snugly covered and sound asleep in the dark green recliner, both legs propped up on the fully extended footrest. They went to the side of the chair, and Gram reached out lovingly and smoothed back a strand of permed, wheat-colored hair from Rachel's forehead, but her breathing remained deep and steady.

Back in the hallway, Lilly was apologetic. "I really should go. I need to change into my uniform and get to the hospital—"

"Don't apologize, whatever you do!" Gram answered. "I think it's wonderful that you stayed with her till we could get here. Rachel talks about this Bible study group all the time, and I can see why. It must be a very special group."

"I don't know about special," Lilly said, smiling, "but we do love each other very much. And we're growing, nearly every week. In fact, we just had someone saved this past weekend, another teenager. We've had several young people do that in the past month or so. And Rachel's been so good—she has the biggest house of any of us, so we've been meeting here. We do appreciate her letting us barge in every week."

Lilly showed them where Rachel's medicine was, along with the care instructions the emergency room had sent home, helped Nikki bring in the suitcases from the Mazda, then left with a hug for each of them. "I'll check back in every day," she promised.

Gram insisted on sleeping in the bed near Rachel, so Nikki ended up in her old bedroom. Tired from four hours of driving, she was asleep within minutes.

Nikki wasn't sure what woke her first the next morning, Rachel's moans as Gram helped her out of the recliner to walk to the bathroom, or Grandpa calling to see how everything was. She stumbled into the hall, rubbing her eyes, and hugged Rachel gingerly, careful not to cause her mother more pain.

Once she was fully awake, Nikki scrambled eggs and fried bacon, then squeezed fresh orange juice, anxious that Rachel have the best breakfast she could come up with. She tried calling Jeff while she was cleaning up the dishes, but there was no answer and his answering machine was turned off.

She ran errands after that, to the drugstore for a new ice pack and to her mother's office at the junior college, lugging home a paper-stuffed briefcase and armloads full of files. Rachel had asked for all her work to be brought home to the house, thinking she could keep up with at least some of her workload there. But by mid-morning, when Nikki finished the errands, Rachel was sound asleep again.

"Shhhh," Gram whispered as Nikki opened the door from the garage. "She's just gone back to sleep. And I want her to stay that way as much as possible, because she's really in a great deal of pain. The swelling just won't go down."

Nikki loaded the dishwasher and turned it on, then settled down at the kitchen table with her homework. She and Gram decided that the school would be much more likely to believe the story of where

Nikki was if it came from an adult. Gram called and began to explain, only to find that Grandpa had already contacted the high school office and had Nikki's assignments e-mailed to Rachel's e-mail address.

Nikki tried Jeff's phone again and again throughout the day, with the same result. Then she worked at her homework for a couple of hours, thinking that it took much longer here, with people from the Bible study and church calling every few minutes. She had to report on Rachel's health so many times she came up with a little set speech, thanking people for calling and explaining why her mother couldn't answer phone calls just then.

She was finally beginning to get into the routine—take a call, do a page of Spanish, take a call, do a page of trig—when the doorbell rang. Nikki went to open the door and found herself staring into a huge pot of purple chrysanthemums.

Behind them stood T.J.

❦ *Sixteen* ❦

T.J. STARED AT NIKKI over the top of the flowers for an instant, then burst out, "What are *you* doing here?"

Nikki stared at him coldly. "I think that should be *my* line, T.J. I used to live here, remember?" She started to close the door on him, but he stopped it with his foot.

"Do you mind, Nikki? I have flowers for your mother." He thrust the chrysanthemums toward her.

"And why on earth would *you* be bringing flowers to my mother?" she asked.

"They're from the Bible study group—"

"Nikki!" Gram's voice sounded from behind her. "What's the problem here? If the young man says he has flowers for Rachel, why on earth are you giving him such a hard time?"

"Yeah," T.J. said, mimicking Gram's words, "why *are* you giving me such a hard time?"

Nikki glared at him, but had to stand aside because Gram was taking the flowers from T.J.'s hands and inviting him in. "Are you delivering these for someone else, dear, or—"

"Oh, no," T.J. said, smiling politely at Gram and ignoring Nikki. "I'm part of the Bible study group now. See, a couple of the guys in the group are my age and we started hanging out together this week. They told me how you can become Christian, and I did."

Oh, brother, Nikki thought, feeling slightly sick at the line he was handing her grandmother. Her feelings about T.J. were so negative that it never even occurred to her that he could possibly be telling the truth.

Gram, however, was having no such problem. She was visibly moved at T.J.'s words, and insisted that he sit down and tell them all about what had happened. "Rachel's sleeping because of the pain medicine, or I'd take you in to see her. But we'd love to hear all about it, wouldn't we, Nikki?"

"Actually, I need to get back to my homework," Nikki said, and headed for the kitchen. She could feel Gram's eyes boring into her back as she left the living room, but she ignored that.

∞

After a while, Nikki heard the front door shut. Then Gram appeared alone in the kitchen doorway.

"Nikki." By the sound of Gram's voice, Nikki knew she had some explaining to do. She sighed and shut her Spanish book.

Gram's voice was dripping disappointment as she began, her hands on her hips. "I don't think I've ever seen you be so rude. Would you mind telling me what that was all about? T.J. seemed like a charming young man, I thought."

"Yeah, he seems like it, all right," Nikki said. "Except you don't know the guy behind all the charm, and I do, unfortunately."

Gram pulled out a chair and settled down across the kitchen table from Nikki, watching her expectantly.

"Gram, I don't mean to be rude to you. But there are—there are *reasons*—why I'd rather not talk about all this, if you don't mind."

Gram's eyes never left Nikki's. "I do mind. It seems to me that something big must be behind all this, and I think I'd like to know what it is. Please, Nikki."

Nikki sighed and looked away, searching for a way to begin gracefully. After a minute she gave up and simply plunged in headfirst, grieving that there was no way to tell Gram who T.J. was without hurting her.

"Gram, T.J. is—he's—Evan's—*father*. His biological father, I mean."

Gram's eyes grew wide, then filled with quick tears. "Oh, Nikki, I had no idea. How awkward for you. Is this the first time you've seen him since you came to live with us?"

Nikki shook her head. "I ran into him in a store down here the other week."

"Does he know about Evan?"

Nikki leaned her elbows on the table and ran her hands through her hair. "I think so. I mean, I'm not really sure, but I suspect he does. I kind of blurted something out when I ran into him, something that made him suspicious. So he went and found Mother at the junior college—he's a freshman there now, I guess—and tried to find a way to contact me. And she gave him our number, in Michigan!" she ended indignantly.

Gram was shaking her head back and forth, making little clucking sounds with her tongue. "And meanwhile, Rachel—who just got her own life straightened out—invites him to Bible study and to church, and he becomes a Christian. How remarkable. Like a chain of dominoes God set in motion, isn't it?"

"Gram! Come on! You don't believe for a minute that he really got saved, do you?" Nikki cried. "T.J. was the fastest talker in town, and a liar and a cheat, too. I wouldn't trust him any further than I could throw him!"

"He was that terrible and you still went out with him?" Gram asked quietly, her hands folded on the oak table before her.

"Okay, so maybe he wasn't *that* bad. But listen, Gram, you don't know this guy. I do."

Gram thought for a moment. "Are you saying that, because he wronged you in the past, he can never change? Is that what you mean?"

Nikki pushed back her chair so quickly that it scraped against the linoleum. Rather than answer the question, she went to the refrigerator and poured herself some orange juice. She stood at the sink drinking it, her back to the table.

Gram's voice, when she spoke again, was soft. "Of course, *I* did wrong, and I changed, with God's help. And *you* did wrong, but you changed, with God's help." She paused. "I have to tell you, Nikki, I found T.J.'s testimony very convincing. Maybe if you'd stayed around to hear it, you would have, too."

Nikki stood staring out the kitchen window a long time, far longer than it took to drink the glass of orange juice. After several minutes of silence, she put her glass in the sink and said, "I'm going to go check on my mother." She left the room without looking at Gram.

Rachel was waking up when Nikki peeked into her bedroom.

"How's it feel?" Nikki asked, going to sit on the bed in front of Rachel.

Rachel smiled sleepily. "I'm so full of pain medicine that I'm not really sure. I don't seem to be feeling much of anything, actually. What time is it?"

When Nikki told her it was 2:00, Rachel groaned. "I can't believe I've wasted 24 hours. And I've got so much to do at school. Did you bring my work home, Nikki?"

Nikki nodded. "Can I get you anything?"

Rachel shook her head, indicating the juice and water and medicine and books which filled the table beside her chair. "I'm think I'm set for life." She laughed and shook her head. "Hard to believe one little fall could result in this." She tugged at the afghan, exposing her foot, then moved her swollen ankle cautiously and winced.

"I think the swelling's finally going down a bit. That has to be a good sign, doesn't it? The doctor said I could sleep in bed tonight if it did, but I still have to have pillows under my foot." She looked up at Nikki and smiled. "In case I didn't say this before—actually, it's hard to remember *what* I've said, with all this medicine in me—I really appreciate you and Mom coming all the way down here. I feel like such a baby to have to ask for help, but—" She stopped in mid-sentence. "Nikki, where did those gorgeous flowers come from? The chrysanthemums? I don't think I've ever seen a plant so loaded with blooms. Did you bring it, sweetie?"

Nikki shook her head. "I wish I'd thought of it, but no, it wasn't me. Sorry."

"Then who?"

"T.J. brought them, from your Bible study group."

A flash of recognition crossed Rachel's face. "That's it! That's what I was supposed to tell you yesterday when I called, but I couldn't remember. T.J. came to the Bible study this week—" Rachel tried to shift her position slightly in the recliner, then groaned— "and some of the guys his age who come talked with him afterwards, and sure enough, he became a Christian. Isn't that *wonderful*, Nikki?"

Nikki nodded. "Wonderful," she said, her voice weak.

"I hope you'll talk to him while you're here, Nikki. There's a lot you don't know about him. It turns out he'd been looking for answers for a long time, but his family had never even been inside a church, as far as he could remember, except on Christmas Eve."

Nikki appeared to be listening as Rachel finished her story, but her thoughts were far away—over a year and a half away, to be precise. The look on T.J.'s face the night she'd become pregnant, the way he looked when he was drunk afterward—Nikki shook her head slightly. *He sure had a strange way of looking for answers*, she thought bitterly.

Later that afternoon, with Rachel watching TV in her room and Gram taking a nap in the guest room, Nikki sat at the kitchen table again trying to catch up on her homework. After half an hour of trying to push thoughts of T.J. away, she finally got up and went to the living room for her mother's Bible, which she'd seen lying on the coffee table. She brought it with her to the kitchen and turned once again to the passage in Romans 12 which had been plaguing her for the last several days.

"Do not repay anyone evil for evil," the verse said. She wondered guiltily if that included rudeness. *"Do not take revenge, my friends, but leave room for God's wrath, for it is written: 'It is mine to avenge. I will repay,' says the Lord."*

See, that's the problem right there, Lord, Nikki prayed. *There sure hasn't been any revenge in T.J.'s life. I've told You before, I'm the one whose entire life got turned upside down. I'm the one who had to move to Michigan and carry the baby and go through labor. And then go through all the pain of giving Evan up for adoption. And what happened to T.J.? Nothing. Absolutely nothing! He stayed here and played soccer and probably got even more popular and dated who knows how many other girls. And went on to college. And now, on top of everything else, he gets to be a Christian, so we just wipe the slate clean, right?*

She realized suddenly why that made her so furious. She didn't *want* T.J. to be forgiven. It was all too easy that way. She wanted him to pay for what they'd done, pay the way she had.

Nikki snapped the Bible shut and dashed away the tears on her cheeks with angry hands. That was how Gram found her a second later when she walked into the kitchen, arms above her head, stretching.

"Oh, I really needed that rest—*Nikki!* What's wrong?"

"He got off scot-free, Gram!" Nikki burst out, not caring whether she made sense to the older woman. "He was just as much a part of it as I was, but I paid the price and T.J. got off totally free. I think this whole forgiveness thing is—is—"

"Outrageous?" Gram supplied the word for her at last and Nikki nodded.

"Exactly! It's outrageous. And now, not only does God let him off the hook, but I'm supposed to do the same."

Gram took the tea kettle to the sink and filled it with water. She put the kettle on the stove and switched the gas to 'high,' then sat down across from Nikki while she waited.

"Forgiveness *is* outrageous, in one sense. But whether that's good or bad seems to depend on which end of forgiveness you're on—the giving end or the receiving end."

Nikki blew her nose and waited, listening.

Gram reached across the table and covered Nikki's hand with her own. "Aren't you glad, when you come asking God's pardon for something wrong, that He forgives you that way? Totally? With no strings attached, no saying, 'Well, you'll have to pay somehow before I can let you off the hook'? Aren't you glad His forgiveness is, as you say, outrageous? I know I am."

"It's not fair for him to get off this way, Gram. Look at everything I went through, and you and Grandpa, too."

Gram shook her head. "No, honey, don't do that—don't try to justify not forgiving by saying your grandfather and I were hurt. You have to concern yourself with *you*, and how you need to respond. And I'll tell you something you may not understand right now. Forgiving may seem to have too high a cost to you. But the cost of *not* forgiving is far, far higher. Bitterness and hatred take an awful toll on a person."

"It's impossible," Nikki said. "I can *never* forgive T.J." She pulled her hand away and blew her nose again.

The kettle began a faint hum, then a quiet whistle which grew to a shriek. Gram got up and switched off the gas. She fixed a cup of tea for herself, and one for Rachel, and put everything on a small tray to take to the bedroom. Before she left the kitchen, she stopped, balancing the tray against the back of the chair across the table from Nikki.

"Forgiving other people only seems impossible when we lose sight of the fact that we're all sinners. Martin Luther said something I need to remind myself of every now and then. He said that 'in the face of God's mercy, we are all beggars.' "

Nikki sat in the quiet of the kitchen after Gram left, listening to the final, dying hiss of the cooling kettle. She could hear Gram and Rachel laughing together in the bedroom, and the sound only served to make her feel more alone than ever.

Her anger at T.J., which had seemed so appropriate up to now, was beginning to feel more like a prison. Deep inside her, something wanted to break out, to surface in the fresh air, but she couldn't seem to find the way to let that happen.

The phone rang at her elbow, startling her out of her thoughts.

"Nikki? Is that you?" Jeff's voice was a welcome sound at first, then she remembered how much explaining she had to do.

"Oh, Jeff, I've been trying to call you all day! I tried to call you back last night, too. Things just went crazy here. My mother—"

"You grandfather told me all about her, Nik," Jeff interrupted. "How's she doing?"

"She's basically been knocked out by the pain medicine, but she's starting to cut back on that now. She thinks the swelling in her ankle's going down, which is really good, but she has to stay off of it for a long time yet. Listen, Jeff, about last night—"

"Yeah, was is something I said?" he joked.

"Come on, Jeff, I'm serious. I just got so upset when my mother told me what happened that I totally—*totally*—forgot you were on the other line. I am really, really sorry."

Jeff hesitated just an instant longer than normal, then said, "It's okay. Don't worry about it."

"You sure?"

" 'Course I am. Look at it this way: It was good for my ego. Every guy should get forgotten on the phone now and then. Keeps him from getting the idea he's too important, you know?"

"Jeff!"

"Hey, relax. I'm kidding," he said, and she was relieved to hear laughter in his voice. "I couldn't let you get off completely—I had to give you a little flak at least."

❧ *Seventeen* ❧

"NIKKI, I GUESS I just don't understand what's going on," Jeff said at last, after they'd talked half an hour. His voice was serious now, all joking gone. "What's going on between us really matters to me. On Saturday, you seemed as excited as me about coming up with ideas about how we can make things better, but now you won't do anything about it."

Nikki was in a bind. To explain the truth to Jeff, she'd have to admit out loud her absolute refusal to even consider forgiving T.J. She knew what Jeff would say about *that*, and it infuriated her.

Jeff's voice was sad, hesitant. "I get the feeling there's more to this than you're telling me, Nik." They were both silent for a moment, then he finished. "How about we leave it this way: Whenever you actually get around to thinking about this, you call me, okay?"

Nikki cringed at his words, wanting to cry out to him to wait, that she'd explain as soon as she could. But how would she explain the hatred that had sprung up in her heart toward T.J.? The desire to pay him back that was now overwhelming even her relationship with the Lord?

Nikki stared miserably at the phone in her hand after Jeff hung up, tears rolling down her cheeks. *For a conversation that started out so good, it sure ended in the pits*, she thought. *Now what do I do?*

When Rachel called to her from the bedroom then, Nikki was

glad for the distraction. She wiped the tears off her cheeks and blew her nose, then went to the doorway of her mother's room. The TV was muted, and it looked as though Gram and Rachel were in the middle of a heated debate.

"Come on in, Nikki," said Rachel, who was finally beginning to look like herself again. "We're taking a vote here, about dinner. I want to order Chinese. Your grandmother, however, thinks the two of you should slave away in the kitchen and do something home-made. *You* get to cast the deciding vote."

Nikki rolled her eyes. "Shrimp egg rolls vs. doing dishes? Sounds like a no-brainer to me. Where's the phone book?"

Rachel had stopped taking all but the minimum dose of pain medicine now, and she was wide awake and growing stir-crazy. "I think I really need to get up for a while. Maybe I'll sit at the dining room table and put my foot up on a chair. Believe me, other parts of my anatomy besides my ankle are starting to hurt from sitting in this recliner for 24 hours." She rubbed her seat, laughing.

Nikki and Gram helped Rachel safely to the dining room and got her seated at the table, her injured ankle propped on a chair. When the Chinese food came, they devoured the egg drop soup and almond chicken and shrimp egg rolls, leaving the table littered with white cardboard take-out containers.

When they finished, Rachel started to stretch—then winced as pain shot through her ankle again. "Okay, okay! I guess I need to sit still. But I'm not going back to that bedroom yet—it's starting to feel like a jail cell. Are you two up for a game?"

Nikki went to the guest room closet and searched through games from Christmases years before, steadfastly putting thoughts of her conversation with Jeff aside so she wouldn't cry. She finally found the game of Clue, the cellophane on the box still unbroken, and carried it back to the dining room. They spent most of the evening deciding who killed whom, with what weapon and where, alternately laughing like kids and sympathizing with Rachel when stabs of pain hit.

∞

Thursday morning, Nikki slept till 9:00. She pulled on a pair of sweats and a t-shirt, then stopped by her mother's room on her way to the kitchen. The purple chrysanthemums sat big and beautiful in the center of Rachel's dresser, doubled in size by their reflection in the mirror, a constant reminder of T.J. that Nikki tried to ignore. Rachel was back in the recliner, watching a mid-morning news program.

"You doing okay, Mom, after being up so long last night?" she asked.

Rachel nodded. "Listen, if I hadn't gotten up, I would have died of boredom," she said. "But I have to admit, my ankle's more swollen again this morning."

"You'd better stay put today then, right?"

Rachel shrugged. "I guess so. Next time we catch Miss Scarlet doing in poor Mr. Boddy with the candlestick, I guess it'll have to be in here!"

They laughed together and Nikki thought how amazing this all was. She couldn't remember ever playing a board game with her mother before, and memories of laughing together were few and far between. She leaned over and kissed Rachel on the forehead.

Rachel looked up, her expression both surprised and pleased. "Now what did I do to deserve that?"

Nikki didn't answer—just patted her shoulder and turned toward the kitchen. She'd been there only a few minutes, it seemed—just long enough to get a bowl of cereal and start pouring milk on it—when a cry from Rachel startled her.

"Nikki! *Nikki! Come here!*"

Nikki nearly dropped the cereal in her haste to set it on the counter, sloshing milk over the edges of the bowl, then ran back down the hall.

"What's wrong?" she cried as she ran. "Did you hurt your—?"

But Rachel was frantically motioning her to be quiet. She pointed at the TV. "*Listen!*"

A reporter stood in front of a brick wall, rain pelting his face as he spoke into the mike. "All we know for sure is that a gunman is holding an unspecified number of students in a room on the other side of the school. We don't know whether or not he's working alone, or whether he's a student or an intruder. To recap what I told you earlier, most of the students were able to evacuate the building when the shots first began, but no one knows exactly what's going on inside that classroom. The door is open a little, police say, enough for the gunman to see down the hall. He threatens anyone who approaches with his gun, and he won't say how many students he has trapped inside. He's also shouting that there are bombs planted around the school. The SWAT team is here and in position, and parents are starting to gather in the parking lot. But for now, it's just another horrible waiting game."

Nikki's first reaction was a kind of general sadness. *Not again*, she thought. *I hope nobody gets hurt or killed this time.*

Then something happened that changed her perspective in an instant. The camera panned across the parking lot and the school beyond, to a scene that was suddenly familiar, and Nikki dropped to a sitting position on the bed as though all the strength had drained from her legs. At the same time, the reporter signed off, saying, "This is John Wiley, reporting to you live from Howellsville High School in Howellsville, Michigan."

"This can't be happening," Nikki cried, feeling sick at her stomach. "It's got to be some kind of a joke—a really *sick* joke."

Rachel stretched out a hand to her and Nikki grasped it hard. Rachel's voice was gentle when she spoke. "I'm afraid it's no joke, Nikki. And I'm so sorry it's happening. It must be unbelievably painful for the people there, but how I thank God that you're here with me, safe and sound!"

Nikki's attention was so riveted on the screen that she hardly heard Rachel's words.

The next few hours were a blur. She wasn't sure when her grandmother came in. She just knew that at some point Gram was sitting there with her on the bed, one arm around her.

One reporter after another checked in, but they all seemed to say the same things over and over. Grandpa called several times, trying to comfort Nikki, but he knew no more there in Michigan than they did here in Ohio, and told them the streets to the high school were blocked off to all but emergency personnel.

"Could you just call Keesha's house, Grandpa?" Nikki pleaded. "Just in case she might have stayed home sick or something?"

He made a soft sound of regret before he answered. "I already did that, honey, as soon as I heard what was going on, but there was no answer."

"Well, could you keep trying? I have to know if she's one of the ones who got out! I mean, maybe she's on her way home right now and just hasn't got there yet."

"I'll keep trying," he assured her.

It was the most miserable of mornings, perched uncomfortably on the edge of her mother's bed, eyes glued to the TV, afraid to leave for even a second in case something should happen.

Gram left long enough to brew a fresh pot of coffee. Even Nikki had a cup, thinking how odd it was that only a few days ago she'd watched Noel drink her coffee and envied her sophistication.

How stupid I was to worry about stuff like that, she thought now, then sat up straight suddenly as another thought occurred to her. "I wonder if Hollis and Noel are in that room!" she said.

Hollis—Nikki couldn't help thinking about how Hollis had acted at lunch and during Current Events class. Though they'd never been friends, she'd begun to see flashes of something different in Hollis recently. Even those brief glimpses had helped her see Hollis as a real person, not just the aloof, intellectual super-student she always appeared to be.

Oh, God, please! she prayed, sipping the bitter black coffee and staring at the TV screen. *Please let Hollis be okay. And Keesha. She was right, I haven't been spending enough time with her. And I never did talk to her about what it really means to be a Christian. I always meant to, but somehow I just never got around to it.*

She tried miserably to pray for them, but found herself at a loss. *How on earth am I supposed to pray for people who might be hostages?* she wondered. That was something she'd never heard covered in youth group.

And Chad—what if he was in there?

At the thought of Chad, Nikki hung her head. All the while they'd been going out together, it had been mostly *her* problems they discussed—the pain she felt over giving up Evan for adoption, the anger at her parents, the depression she was fighting. Sometimes Chad had talked about himself, when she'd urged him to do so. *But I was so wrapped up in myself, I hardly ever did.*

There had been more than just hurt in his words in the cafeteria last Monday. For just one moment, it was as though he'd pulled back a curtain and she had seen that he was in some kind of terrible depression. Then he'd tried to hide it, the way he always did. But— amazingly for him—he had even asked to talk with her. *And I basically blew him off.* No matter how much he aggravated and even angered her, Nikki knew she couldn't help caring what happened to Chad. They'd been too close for that.

Incredibly, all the stuff that had seemed so important just the day before—relationships, homework, grades, who drove what car and who wore what clothes—mattered not at all now. In the face of possible death, there was only one thing that mattered. Nikki felt as though she was seeing clearly for the first time.

I especially pray for Keesha and Chad, Lord. I had more chances to tell them about You than I did anyone else. And I blew it. I blew it. Please don't let them be trapped in that room with the gunman. Let them be out of there, somewhere safe and sound.

She prayed over and over. When Gram put a chicken salad sandwich in front of her sometime around noon, Nikki took it and mumbled thanks, then set the plate on the bed in front of her and promptly forgot all about it.

When at last the phone rang and Grandpa asked to speak to her, Nikki was ecstatic, sure that her prayers had been answered at last.

"Grandpa! Did you get Keesha? Is she all right?"

His voice held some joy, but not as much as Nikki would have hoped. "Yes, I did. And yes, she is. I just talked to her at her house. She's one of the ones who got away this morning when they first evacuated the school. But Nikki—" he stopped, and she thought she heard him swallow hard.

"What? What's wrong?" she cried. "Grandpa, tell me!"

"Keesha says—now, I don't have any way of verifying this, honey—but she says that the gunman is a student you know. She says it's it's—Chad."

Nikki had to get out of the room.

It made no sense, because she wanted more than anything to be right there in front of the TV, to know the exact minute anything happened.

But she had to get air, right away. There was a strangling feeling in her throat, as though something was cutting off her breath. All she could see was Chad's face on Monday in the cafeteria. His words echoed over and over in her mind. *You were about the only one I could ever talk to around here, Nikki.* And she had been so wrapped up in herself, so busy trying to make him understand she didn't want to go out with him, she'd missed the importance of what he was saying.

Nikki jumped to her feet, toppling the plate and sandwich onto the floor, but she couldn't stop. She ran down the hall and out the front door, as though trying to put as much distance as possible between herself and the phone.

"Keesha says she saw Chad when he came into school with the gun," Grandpa had said on the phone. *"She was on her way to the library and saw him from behind. Now, Nikki, sweetheart, you keep in mind that Keesha may be wrong. I mean, maybe she just thought it was him, or—"*

But Nikki had stopped listening then. Keesha had a wild imagination, she knew, but there would have been no mistaking Chad's nearly white-blond hair for someone else's. No other guy in school had hair like that.

She left the house without a jacket, but it was more than the chilly autumn air that made her tremble as she ran. The sky was brilliant blue, the sun at nearly its highest point in the sky, but the beauty seemed to mock the darkness inside her.

She couldn't help thinking about all the other school shootings in the past year. The students who did the shootings sometimes died, either killing themselves or getting shot by police officers trying to rescue hostages.

A desperate sense of panic welled up inside her so that she wanted to scream, right there on the street. *I couldn't stand Chad sometimes, Lord, You know that. But I never wanted him to die! He drove me nuts, I admit that, and You know that usually, he was trying to. But still, I should have made time to talk to him when he asked me to. I could see something was wrong, the crazy way he's been acting. I could see he needed to talk, but I didn't do anything. God, please! Please do something. Please get him out of this, somehow.*

If he didn't die, he would probably go to prison. And in one way, that seemed almost as bad. Maybe worse. *Being shut up like that for years and years and years—*

Nikki shuddered, running faster and faster as though she was being pursued. A cramp grew and grew in her right side, until finally it forced her to a walk. She raised both hands over her head, trying to ease the pain. She looked around and realized that she was at least two miles from home. She turned back reluctantly, but with no other choice.

The running had drained her of some of the panic, and she tried to pray again as she walked. *Oh, God, please, please—*she wished so much that she knew more about prayer, knew what to pray *for.* But each sentence seemed to dwindle to an inarticulate plea for help, more felt than thought.

She was totally played out by the time she got within a block of her mother's house. All she could think of by then was getting inside to sit down, of having a huge drink of anything cold.

Which may have explained in part what happened when she saw T.J. in the driveway.

The door of his late model, black Grand Am was open and he was getting out. It was the worst possible timing. Nikki didn't miss a beat. She walked across the lawn until she was nearly nose-to-nose with him, close enough to see the cut ends of blond whiskers scattered across his chin.

Her voice was low and intense. "What is it about *go away* that you don't understand, T.J.? Don't come back again while I'm here, understand? I don't want to talk about what happened between us. *Ever*." She whirled around and walked toward the door.

"Nikki, we're going to have to talk about this sooner or later!" he shouted after her "Besides, I didn't come to talk about what happened between us! I came to talk about the baby!"

Nikki slammed the front door behind her, as though his last words hadn't registered. But she was only pretending.

❦ *Eighteen* ❦

GRAM AND RACHEL were still in the bedroom, right where they'd been when she left. Gram's face was a study in relief when she saw Nikki return, and she moved as though to get up and hug her. But Nikki motioned to her to stay where she was.

"Anything happen while I was gone?" Nikki asked.

Rachel shook her head back and forth. "Just that Keesha called a few minutes ago. She said she got the number from your grandfather and wanted to let you know she's all right," Rachel said.

Nikki picked up the phone and touched in Keesha's number, but got a busy signal. "She'll probably be on the phone the rest of the day, if I know Keesha. Why'd she wait so long to call, anyway?"

"She said she'd been on the phone with relatives ever since she got home."

As always when Nikki was in turmoil, a sudden longing to tell Jeff about the whole situation overwhelmed her. She punched in his number, but got the answering machine. "Jeff," she told the machine, "this is Nikki. Could you call me here in Ohio at my mother's as soon as you can? I really—" her voice broke on the word "—I really need to talk to you."

She disconnected, then dialed Keesha again. This time, she actually got through. "Oh, Keesha, I'm so relieved to hear your voice!" she said when Keesha answered. "I was so afraid this morning that

134

you were in that room—that you might get—"

"Thanks, Nik. I'm okay. But did your grandfather tell you? About Chad, I mean?"

"Yeah," Nikki said, her voice almost a whisper. "Keesha, are you *sure*? I mean, like, absolutely sure?"

Keesha sighed, as though she wished she didn't have to answer the question. "Nikki, is there another guy in the whole school who looks like Chad? Or walks like him, or—"

"It's okay. You don't have to explain. I was just hoping. Keesha, did anybody say anything about *why* he's doing this?"

Keesha made a derisive sound, half sigh, half laugh. "Nikki, come on! Does anybody ever know why Chad Davies does *anything*?"

"Yeah, I guess you're right," Nikki said, but the picture of Chad's face when he asked her to talk flashed across her mind. *Maybe I know. Maybe, if I'd talked to him more*—"Any idea who else is in that room with him?" Nikki asked.

"Not a clue. Everything just went wild when he fired those first shots. People went running everywhere, trying to get out any door they could, Nik. It was like something from a movie. You wouldn't believe how scared everybody was, even some of the teachers."

"Did he—hit anybody?" Nikki asked, dreading Keesha's answer.

"No, he just shot out windows. You know those big ones in the front lobby? Announcements were just starting, and we could all hear the shots over the speaker. At first, we thought it was some kind of recorded background for a class announcement—you know how they do those crazy ones, sometimes, to sell stuff? Then all of a sudden Mr. Peabody comes on and starts saying, 'Evacuate the school, evacuate the school.' We all just sat there for a minute like zombies, wondering if this was a joke, and then there were *more* shots, and Mr. Peabody says, 'We have an emergency here. Evacuate the school *immediately*. Do not use the lobby doors. I repeat, do not use the lobby doors.'"

Nikki tried to imagine the scene Keesha was describing at Howellsville High, but failed. "Was it bad getting out?" she asked.

"*Bad?* Nik, it was like a stampede! And all the time, Peabody's yelling, 'Don't use the lobby doors!', so everybody headed down toward the gym entrance. We had to go right out in the pouring rain. You should've seen Ms. Mendoza—she was like the only person who stayed cool. She stood right in the middle of the hall directing traffic, like a cop. It was a good thing, though. If she didn't, I think somebody would've got trampled, you know? The whole scene was like, just total *bedlam!*"

Keesha filled in a few more details, but Nikki had heard enough. She felt sick to her stomach just picturing it. And worst of all was knowing that Chad was at the center of it all.

Nikki was growing more and more anxious to talk to Jeff, but she knew there was one important topic she hadn't covered with Keesha yet. When she could break in without being too obvious, she finally brought the conversation around to what was pressing on her mind. "Listen, Keesha, Jeff's s'posed to call any minute, so I think I better get off soon. You sure you're okay?"

"Yeah, I'm all right. It just feels like we're all stuck in this really wild nightmare. Like if we just wait a minute, we'll wake up and it'll all be gone."

"Keesha, before I get off—can we get together and do some serious talking when I get home?"

"So what are we doing right now?" Keesha asked.

"Not about stuff like this. Remember how you said I never really talked to you about what I believe? About being a Christian, I mean?"

"Nik, I told you, I prayed that prayer—"

"Well, when I get back, could we just talk? Right away?"

Keesha hesitated, but Nikki refused to let her off the hook. "See, when I first heard the news today and I thought you might be in that room, or shot in the hall or something, I realized that I've never really talked to you about the one thing that matters more than anything else. And I want to make sure I do, okay?"

Keesha finally agreed, then Nikki got off the phone and dialed Jeff's number. His answering machine clicked on again and Nikki repeated her message in frustration.

The afternoon passed with agonizing slowness. Gram went in

and out of the bedroom, leaving to start a load of laundry for Rachel, then to start dinner. After each task, she perched for a few minutes on the bed beside Nikki to make sure she hadn't missed anything.

Nikki gathered her homework from the kitchen table and took it to Rachel's room, but it sat undone on the bed beside her. She thought about the students trapped in that classroom and felt sick. But when she thought about Chad, the knot in her stomach grew tighter and tighter as the hours passed.

None of this made sense to her. *Chad's mad, sure. Mad at his mother for leaving, mad at his father for all the drinking.* But there had to be something more. Chad had been dealing with the situation for a couple years now, as near as Nikki could tell.

Chad's too smart to do something like this. Something that'll only make everything worse. She thought about that for a second, then shook her head. *Unless he's drunk.* She'd seen him drunk before, and she knew it would take more than that to make him hold people hostage. Besides, he'd never be able to control them if he was in that condition.

There was still a piece of the puzzle missing, she thought, wracking her brain to figure out what it was. *Something must have happened to push him over the edge.* Was that what he'd wanted to talk to her about?

At 2:00, Keesha called back, her words tumbling out so rapidly Nikki could hardly understand her at first. "Nikki! *Noel's* in that room with Chad! I haven't found out yet who the other people are, but Noel's in there for sure! I just heard."

Nikki tried to fight off the feeling of unreality that seemed to wrap itself around her. The whole situation seemed more and more like a nightmare, as Keesha had said—something that couldn't really be happening. If only they could all wake up!

"Thanks, Keesha," she said finally, after they'd talked for a few minutes. "I appreciate you letting me know. Call me if you find out about anybody else in there, okay?"

They'd hardly hung up when the phone rang again. It was

Grandpa. "Nikki?" he asked. "Someone named Hollis just called and wants you to call her back. I have her number here." He read off the number, then asked, "Are you going to be all right, honey? I can't even imagine how you must feel."

Nikki felt her eyes fill with tears at his kindness. The moment he hung up she punched in all but the last digit of Hollis's number, then waited till she was sure her voice was steady to finish dialing.

"Hollis?" she said. "This is Nikki. My grandfather said you called."

Hollis went straight to the point, as always. "Nikki, are you praying?"

"What?"

"I said, 'Are you *praying*?'" she repeated, as though it was the most natural question in the world.

"About what's going on at school, you mean?"

"What else? You said you believed in God, and that He can change things, so I wanted to make sure you're praying."

"Well, sure I am. But I'm not the only one who can pray about this, Hollis. You could—"

"Naturally. I thought about what you said about God, and I decided I need to talk to you more about this. But until I can, I didn't think it'd do any harm for me to pray. I just wanted to make sure you were, too. Noel's going to need all the prayer she can get, because she'll never forgive herself for this."

Nikki frowned. Hollis's words made no sense at all.

"Would you repeat that? What you just said about Noel?"

"I said Noel's never going to forgive herself."

"Wait a minute, Hollis. I don't get what you're saying. Keesha just told me Noel's one of the people Chad has trapped in the classroom. What's she got to forgive herself for?" Nikki asked.

"Come on, Nikki. You *have* to know."

"Know what?" Nikki asked, feeling extraordinarily stupid.

Hollis gave a disgusted sigh. "Nikki, you need more practice putting two and two together. Chad and Noel started going out together in August. Remember?"

"I never knew that! I was away with my aunt in Virginia in August. And I've never seen them together at school—"

"She broke it off by the time school started, so a lot of people didn't know," Hollis continued. "She said he was crazy, always talking about suicide and stuff. But come on, Nikki. You must've guessed something was up when Noel kept pushing to talk about abortion every chance she got—first to you, and then in Current Events and all. So put two and two together."

"*Noel* was the one who wanted to talk about abortion? She said it was your idea," Nikki said, trying to make light of the fact that she understood no more about the situation now than she had when Hollis first called.

"That was all just a front, Nikki, because Noel didn't want anybody besides me to know she was pregnant. She finally had the abortion Tuesday night. Chad kept telling her not to. He said if she'd just have the baby, they could adopt it out, but you know Noel—there was no way she'd do the whole pregnancy thing. Chad kept saying she should talk to you because you'd been through all this and you knew the truth about abortion. When he found out she went ahead and did it anyway, he went on an all-night binge. He was *nuts*, Nikki, believe me."

"Wait a minute, here, Hollis. Are we talking about the same Chad?" Nikki asked. "Just explain to me why on earth he'd care whether or not Noel had an abortion."

"I don't know, Nikki. He kept telling Noel he wasn't going to be around long and he didn't need one more thing on his conscience. She said it wouldn't be on his, it'd be on *hers*, but he said it was his baby, too, and he had to stop her if he could."

❧ *Nineteen* ❧

NIKKI WAS STILL REELING from Hollis's revelation when she noticed a distinct change on the TV screen. Suddenly one of the on-the-scene reporters was back, reading from his notes as though he hadn't had time to prepare. His mouth was moving, but no sound could be heard.

"Come on, come *on!*" she cried in frustration, her stomach knotting as she waited for the station to correct the audio problem. "How do people ever learn to read lips, anyway?" she fumed. "I can't tell a single thing he's saying." But when the audio finally came through, Nikki was stunned at what she heard.

"—the last 30 minutes, officers finished their sweep of the school building with dogs trained to sniff for explosives. No bombs were found. Once the sweep was completed, and they determined that the student gunman was acting alone, the SWAT team moved in.

"It was all over in a matter of minutes after that. I understand there was a brief period of gunfire, but the student was no match for the highly trained SWAT team members. At this point, only the student who did the shooting appears to be injured, and that happened when he tried to turn his gun on himself. The report is that he's confessed to both acts of vandalism in the last week—the spray-painting and setting the fire. All the students held in the classroom are safe. I repeat, all the students who were held hostage in the classroom have now been released and are with the police."

A wave of relief washed over Nikki, leaving her limp. She fell back on her mother's bed with a huge sigh, yet tears were running down her cheeks as she thought of Chad, locked in his prison of hatred and bitterness. What had happened with his parents wasn't his fault. His reaction to what they'd done was wrong, sure. And if what Hollis said was true, then he'd made another wrong choice with Noel.

But Nikki understood all too well how it felt to make wrong choices and have your whole world fall in on you. She felt sick at the thought of Chad being in that kind of trouble, even though what he had done deserved punishment. The police would have taken him to the hospital for now, she knew, but she wasn't exactly sure what would happen after that. The county jail? The prison? She shuddered at the thought.

I have to go back there and talk to Chad, she realized suddenly. *Maybe there's some way I could help.* She could visit him, wherever they'd locked him up.

And what would you say to him? The question echoed in her head, in tones she was beginning to recognize.

I'd tell him about You, Lord. About how we all mess up. But that he could be forgiven—

And what exactly are you planning to tell him about forgiveness, the voice asked again, *when you won't even speak to T.J.?*

Nikki thought of a hundred excuses, but now there was only a silence to throw them into. A huge, inpenetrable silence. All the excuses in the world would make no more impact on that silence than pebbles tossed into an ocean.

By dinner time, Nikki had given up leaving messages for Jeff. Wherever he was, he hadn't returned her calls or given the slightest attention to her pleas to talk. She wondered if he was far more upset with her than he'd let on. Maybe he was even thinking about breaking up with her.

Gram and Nikki helped Rachel to the kitchen for dinner. Afterwards they sat a long time around the table, sipping hot chocolate and rehashing the day's events. Eventually Nikki sent Rachel and

Gram off to watch a PBS nature special, offering to clean up the kitchen herself. At first she thought she'd welcome the time alone to sort things out. Before long, though, she felt the silence around her grow deafening.

I'm going to have to talk to T.J., she finally admitted, scrubbing at a ring of dried chocolate inside her mother's mug.

I can't figure things out with Jeff until I do. And now, I can't even help Chad unless I get this straightened out first. And then there were Keesha and Hollis. She knew now she wouldn't be much good to anyone until she could get past the issue of T.J.

Nikki loaded the last of the silverware into the dishwasher, then poured in the soap and turned it on. She searched the kitchen for any last bit of work she could use to put off what she had to do. But the sink was scoured, the counters gleaming. She sighed and reached for the phone. It was all too easy to remember T.J.'s number.

She had to give her name when T.J.'s mother answered. "Just tell him it's Nikki, okay? He'll know who I am."

T.J. made no secret of his surprise when he heard her request. "You want me to come over there? Now?"

Nikki rolled her eyes and very nearly hung up, but she knew she had to see this through. "Can you, please?"

"Give me 15 minutes."

Nikki couldn't resist changing her t-shirt for a deep blue pullover sweater, then decided at the last minute to put on mascara and blush. She no longer had any interest in impressing T.J., but she needed the self-confidence of knowing she looked good. On her way back to the living room, she stopped by her mother's room.

"Would you mind giving me some time alone in the living room?" she asked Rachel and Gram. "I need to talk to someone who's coming over, someone who's—" She stopped, floundering. How was she supposed to describe who T.J. was? He wasn't a friend, that was for sure. She gave up and just said it straight out. "Actually, it's—it's T.J. that's coming."

Gram smiled at her, and Nikki knew she was cheering her on. Rachel made a surprised little "o" with her mouth, then nodded. "It's fine with me. Just so you know that Lilly called and said she's dropping by later to check on me."

"That's fine. I'm sure we won't be long," Nikki told her.

By the time T.J. arrived, she had turned on the lamps in the living room, and was as ready as she could be for what promised to be one of the toughest conversations of her life.

When T.J. strode up the sidewalk, Nikki opened the front door and motioned him in silently. Once he was inside she shut the door behind her—then leaned against it, facing him.

"I'll be honest with you, T.J. I've done everything I can to avoid you, and I still don't want to have this conversation. But I have to."

He pressed his lips together and shrugged off his brown leather jacket. "I deserve that, I guess."

Nikki nodded toward the couch and T.J. walked across the room and sat down, laying the jacket beside him. Nikki sank into the leather recliner and crossed her arms over her chest, facing T.J. across the coffee table.

"All right. You keep saying you want to talk to me. So this is your chance, whatever you want to say," she told him. She knew her words sounded belligerent, but she had to keep up her guard against T.J. She waited for his answer, remembering how sarcastic he could be.

T.J. leaned forward, hands folded loosely between his knees, his face intent. "Nikki, I'm sorry."

His voice was low, troubled-sounding, and it caught Nikki completely off guard. She waited silently for him to continue.

"Back when I was on the soccer team, I knew I drank too much whenever I was with those guys." He put out both hands, palms up. "The weird thing was, I—I didn't even like to drink. I just started doing it to be one of the guys. So, when this all happened between you and me—"

Nikki was amazed to hear T.J. stumble, searching for words. She relaxed her crossed arms and slid her hands to the arms of the recliner.

"—I mean, when we were together that night, I was really

drunk. I told you before, I don't remember much about what happened."

She gave a short laugh. "Well, I do."

T.J. closed his eyes, tight, for second, and Nikki could tell her words had hit their target.

"Yeah, I guess you do. I didn't know you got pregnant, not for a long time, you know?" He raised his eyebrows, waiting for an answer, but she said nothing. She wasn't about to make this any easier for him.

"Nikki, I know I acted like a real jerk after that night. Like I said, I couldn't really remember what happened. But the day after Lauren's party, the guys all made a big deal of how long we were in the bedroom together, so I pretty much figured out what went on. After that, it was easier just to ignore you and pretend I didn't care than to face you. Nikki, I—I used to see you in the hall at school and your eyes—well, they always looked so hurt. It used to kill me to see you, but I was scared. I didn't have a clue what to do."

T.J. looked down at the carpet between his feet. "Then there were rumors when you didn't come back to school last year, but nobody knew for sure what happened. I just kept telling myself things, like 'Girls don't get pregnant the first time,' and 'If she is, it probably isn't mine'—"

Nikki pulled herself up straight in the chair and glared at him. "That's really low, T.J."

He shook his head quickly. "I know, I know. People tell themselves some pretty stupid things when they're trying to get out of something like this." He ducked his head for a minute, lacing and unlacing his fingers. "It didn't work, anyway. I can tell you that last year wasn't exactly the best year of my life. It may have looked like it, on the surface, but inside this thing kept eating at me. And I was doing other stuff I'd just as soon forget, too. I started partying practically all the time, because when I was out with the guys, drinking, I could forget. And after a while, I did forget, kind of. I'd been telling myself it wasn't true for so long that I almost started believing it." He looked up at her. "That's why it hit me so hard when I saw you at the 7-Eleven."

Nikki still said nothing, but this time it was because she was so amazed at what she was hearing. She had never seen T.J. vulnerable like this before. The words from Romans that had haunted her, " '*It is mine to avenge; I will repay,' says the Lord*," seemed to be coming true right before her eyes.

"It almost seemed like us meeting at the 7-Eleven was more than just an accident, you know?" he asked.

"What do you mean?" Nikki asked.

T.J. sighed. "My life was pretty much just trash by then. The drinking, the partying—I was into a lot of stuff and I didn't know how to quit. Then, when I saw you, and you made that crack about being pregnant, I knew I'd just been fooling myself. This may sound crazy, but I'd even started praying for help. I didn't know what else to do. But I wanted to see if I could make things right with you, somehow, so I found your mother—I knew she taught at the junior college, so that wasn't hard. I just didn't expect her to be so nice to me. And I sure didn't expect her to invite me in last week—they were having Bible study here that night—and as soon as I heard what they were talking about and studying, and how they prayed, I knew they might be able to help."

He stopped and looked at her, as though wondering if she would understand. "My mother told me you became a Christian," Nikki said.

T.J. looked her directly in the eye. "I did, Nikki. I don't know if you'll understand this, but . . . " He shrugged one shoulder.

"I understand. Last year, after Evan was born, the same thing happened to me."

"Evan? That's his name?" T.J.'s eyes widened and he leaned forward. "Could you—Nikki, would you tell me about him?"

Nikki was taken back by the sudden intensity of his voice. She'd always thought of T.J. as being out for only himself. The things he'd told her in the last few minutes had changed her perception of him a little, but this turned it completely upside down.

"You really want to know?" she asked.

T.J. rolled his eyes. "Nikki, don't you hear me? What d'you want me to do—*beg?*"

Nikki shook her head. "No, I just didn't expect you to—to care, that's all."

T.J. winced. "I can see why you wouldn't. But guys have feelings, too, you know. I mean, this is my *son* we're talking about. Where is he? Can I see him? When I found out you were here last night, I thought maybe he—"

Nikki remembered that T.J. had no idea of all that had happened in the past year. There was no way to cushion what she had to tell him, and her lower lip trembled as she said the words: "T.J., Evan has a new family. I gave him up for adoption."

T.J. sagged against the back of the couch, staring at her, and Nikki was instantly reminded of the day she'd watched him miss the goal kick that decided the soccer championship. When he spoke, his voice was ragged. "Is he somewhere far away?"

Nikki hesitated, and a sudden chill ran through her from head to foot. She'd seen a TV movie once about a birth father who found out about his child and had an adoption overturned. Along with the fear, she felt the sharp-edged jab of guilt. *I never even thought about letting T.J. in on the adoption decision. I thought he wouldn't even care—I thought he just used me and then threw me away without another thought.* But T.J. was changing, almost right in front of her eyes.

"I don't think I ought to answer that," she said at last.

He spoke again, and in his anger Nikki saw a flash of the old, insolent T.J. "Whether you tell me or not, I can find out, Nikki! The courthouse has all the records and I can get a lawyer and—"

He stopped abruptly, then slammed his fist into his palm. "No. *No!* This is the way I used to act, but I'm a Christian now, Nikki. I don't want to push people around like that anymore." He got up from the couch and circled the coffee table that separated them, then sat on the edge of it, close enough that their knees almost touched.

"Nikki, listen to me, please. I've been trying to figure out how to ask you to forgive me. You don't trust me, and I understand that— I haven't given you any reason to. So let me start all over again, here. I'm officially asking you to forgive me. I can't even imagine what it was like for you, being pregnant and having the baby and all. And I won't ask you again where he is. Sometime in the future, when you see that I'm not out to kidnap him or do something else crazy like that, then maybe you'll tell me on your own. But for now, do you think you could just tell me the basic stuff, like, when his birthday is? If he's healthy?"

Nikki swallowed hard, weighing his request. T.J. must have mistaken her silence for a refusal, because at last he said, "Could I maybe just—see a picture of him, then? If you have one?" and his voice was quiet and defeated.

Do not repay evil for evil. The phrase ran over and over in her mind like a tape loop, and she had a sudden glimpse into how high and thick the wall of bitterness and resentment she'd built against T.J. was. *Help me, Lord,* she thought. *Help me now, please, because there's no way I can get over this wall myself.* But the answer she heard deep inside her was unmistakeable. She had to take the first step herself.

She opened her mouth and nothing came out. She tried again, with all her might, and finally managed to say, "I have a picture in my purse. I'll go get it." She began to cry then, trying to hide the tears as she left the room. But she couldn't tell whether the tears were from the sudden light she had seen spring into T.J.'s eyes at her answer, or from the sensation inside her that the wall was crumbling at last.

❧ *Twenty* ❧

NIKKI WATCHED T.J. pore over Evan's picture for several minutes, amazed at the sensation of peace that washed over her once she told T.J. she forgave him. Forgiving him had seemed a mountain too massive to climb, but now she wished she'd done it long ago. She told him a little about Evan's adoptive parents, without mentioning names or telling him where they lived, and he listened intently.

There was the sense of a chapter ending as they talked, and Nikki felt as though a huge weight had finally rolled off her. She knew the ties between them could never be totally severed, not after they had created a child together. That responsibility would always be there. But the crushing weight of hatred and bitterness, the desire to make T.J. pay for hurting her—she had finally been able to let go of that.

Then a knock at the door unsettled everything. "Come in!" Nikki called, expecting Lilly. But when the door opened, she was startled to see it wasn't Lilly at all, but Jeff.

His glance flew from Nikki to T.J., sitting almost knee to knee, poring over the picture in T.J.'s hand, and his eyebrows rose in question.

Nikki jumped to her feet and hurried to Jeff's side. "What are you doing here?" she cried. "I've been trying to call you all day to tell you what's been going on back home—"

He smiled down into her eyes and gave her a quick hug, the kind he'd give to any friend in trouble. "I know. As soon as I heard the news, I figured you could probably use some company, so I just jumped in the truck and drove down." He reached back and closed the door behind him. "Sounds like it's all over now, though. I heard on the news that the kid with the gun was taken into custody just a little while ago, right?"

Nikki nodded, and she could tell by the look in his eyes that he hadn't yet heard who the gunman was. She started to blurt it out, then decided to wait till they were alone.

"I'm just so grateful you came," she said. "I can't believe you took the time to come all the way down here!" She longed for a hug that was far less friend-like, then remembered they were supposed to be working through guidelines for things like this and stepped back a little. At the same time, T.J. cleared his throat and Nikki remembered he was there.

Nikki turned and introduced him reluctantly. And in the second it took to mention T.J.'s name, a shadow seemed to cross Jeff's face, and his smile shrank to a straight line.

T.J. stuck out his hand to Jeff, but Jeff hesitated. Nikki could see him struggle for a second before he finally reached out and shook hands. The three of them sat together then for five minutes or so, talking the way people do when they first meet, about inconsequential things—basketball at U of M, soccer at the junior college where T.J. went.

Anything to keep from mentioning what's really going on here, Nikki thought. She watched Jeff with concern. He was saying all the right words, but his voice was unusually quiet—as though talking to T.J. took more effort than he could muster.

At last, Rachel called from the bedroom. "Is Lilly here yet, Nikki? I thought I heard the door a while ago."

Jeff got to his feet. "I should go in and say hello to your mother, Nik. I want to see how she's feeling, anyway."

Once they were alone again, T.J. picked up the picture of Evan from where he'd set it on the end table. He held it out to her. "He's— he's great, Nikki. I wish I could've known him, but it's too late for that, I guess." He looked down at the floor between them. "I made the most incredible mess out of this and I'm sorry. I know I said it before, but I just want to make sure you know." He looked into her eyes and waited.

"I do, T.J. And I'm sorry, too. You didn't do this alone."

"Do you think you can ever really forgive me?" He looked down again, as though too much hung on the question to face it head on.

"I do, T.J. I can, and I do."

He stood then, and put his hand out to her. "Thanks, Nikki. I guess I'll get going then. I just want you to know that you have my word that I'll never do anything to disrupt Evan's life."

Nikki stood, too, and took his hand for just a second as she thanked him. Then she added, "You know, I get new pictures from Evan's parents every six months. If you'd like, T.J., I could send you copies."

T.J.'s eyes filled suddenly, and he ducked his head, nodding. "Thank you. I'd like that a lot."

∽

After T.J. left, Nikki went looking for Jeff. Rachel and Gram had already filled him in about who the gunman had been. Nikki could see the shocked look in his eyes.

"Jeff, could we go talk in the kitchen?" she asked. "I really need a cup of hot chocolate or tea or something."

Seated at the kitchen table a few minutes later, Jeff rubbed his forehead with his thumb and forefinger, as though trying to figure it all out. "But *why*? What would make Chad do something like this? I know he's got a hair-trigger temper, and he drinks, but still—"

"That's part of the reason I need to get home tomorrow," Nikki said. "Chad told me this week he wanted to talk to me, and I just put him off, you know? I mean, with Chad it was always hard to tell whether he was serious or not. But apparently he was, because today I found out something else."

While she made hot chocolate for both of them, Nikki told Jeff about Noel's abortion. He seemed totally absorbed in what she was saying, but underneath, Nikki couldn't help sensing that he was just as glad to have their conversation stay on the topic of other people.

"And you really think Noel's abortion had something to do with this, Nik?" he asked, incredulous. "You think a guy like Chad would even care?"

Nikki shrugged and set the mugs on the table. "Well, Hollis sure thinks so. All I know is, Chad's had one loss after another in the last few years—his mother leaving, his father leaving in a different way, by being drunk all the time—and now this. And he never really seemed to deal with any of it, you know? At first, he just kept getting angrier and angrier inside. But lately, it was like he was giving up. Jeff," she said quietly, "Hollis said he was talking about *suicide*, and he said he didn't want the death of this baby on his conscience."

"Wow! Chad didn't strike me as the kind of guy who would think twice about something like abortion," Jeff said, stirring the dark liquid in his cup.

Nikki stared into her own cup. Her eyes were fixed on the reflection of the ceiling light in the chocolate, but she saw T.J.'s eyes brimming with tears. "Yeah, up until today, that's what I would've said, too. I just think there was a lot more going on inside Chad than anybody ever saw. I know there was in T.J."

She tried to describe in just a few words what had happened during her time with T.J. that evening. But when she looked up she could tell that, even though Jeff's eyes were intent on hers, his thoughts were not totally with her.

"Jeff?"

He came back with a start, and set his mug down on the table with a little *thud.* "I'm sorry, Nik. I know this is all really important to you, but—"

"Jeff, *you're* important to me."

His eyes searched her face, and he bit at his bottom lip for a second before he started. "It's just that—I mean, I had no idea," was the first thing he said.

"No idea about what?" she asked.

"When you told me last year that you were pregnant, I remember feeling really furious at whoever the guy was, like I wanted to beat him to a pulp. But that was all he was—just some faceless guy. But then, when I got here tonight—" Jeff shifted uncomfortably in his chair before he tried again.

"I mean, there he was. A real person. A real guy who—who—actually slept with you." He pushed the mug of chocolate away from him. "Nikki, I've seen what you've been through over the past year and a half—"

"And you've walked through this whole thing with me, Jeff. I could never have survived it without you."

"I'm not out to make you feel any more pain, that's for sure. But Nik, when I saw him, everything kind of turned upside down for me. I don't even know how to put it in words, except that I feel like I lost something to him, something that would've really mattered to me."

He glanced up at her, then away. "What I mean is, even if we get married someday—and that's what I want, Nikki, 'cause I love you. I think I've always loved you, always wanted you in my life. But if we do, it will never—" his voice cracked, and he stopped, unable to go on.

The truth of what he must be feeling dawned on Nikki for the first time, and her voice was flat as she said it for him. "I gave T.J. what I can never give you." She struggled to hold back her emotion. "My being a—a virgin, right?"

Jeff was silent, but Nikki's thoughts screamed what she'd been too blind to see. *All along, I've been thinking that what happened between T.J. and me was just about us—me, T.J., the baby. And that was bad enough.* But as she stared at Jeff's face, it dawned on her for the first time that it had been about far more.

T.J. took it so casually, she thought, remembering that night. To T.J.'s crowd, having sex had been something to snicker about, an accepted part of just about every party. *But to Jeff—and to me, too, now—it means something totally different. Something really, really important, that God meant for just the two of us to share.*

She watched him sit across the table from her, his eyes averted, running his thumb up and down the handle of his mug. And she saw that, when she slept with T.J., she'd stolen something precious from Jeff, or whoever her husband would someday be.

For a minute, Nikki felt she might drown in regret. But if she'd learned anything in the past year, it was that regret could smother her ability to make the right choices for the future.

God has forgiven me, she reminded herself, hanging on with all her might to what she knew to be true, though she'd seldom felt less forgiven.

Nikki reached across the kitchen table and touched Jeff's fingers. "Jeff, I'm sorry. That doesn't sound anywhere near adequate, I know. But I can't change what happened, not now. I'm just so sorry."

Jeff shook his head and motioned her to stop. "Don't, Nik! You know we've settled this all before—" He broke off and looked at her, as though unsure of where to go from there.

"Jeff, you have to know, this is what I've been struggling with. This is why I couldn't come up with any guidelines about our relationship. You thought it didn't matter to me, but it does. But T.J.'s been calling and that was all I could think about. It was really important for me to have to face him, to forgive him. Because now I'm free of that. I'm free to build the best possible relationship I can with you."

Nikki saw a glimmer of hope began to shine in Jeff's eyes at her words. And in her own heart, the kind of relationship she wanted to have with him began to take shape.

Jeff leaned forward across the table. "I didn't make it any easier for you, did I? Trying to push you into doing what I thought was right for us and getting upset when you didn't move as fast as I thought you should—" He broke off and shook his head as though in wonder. "Sometimes I can be a jerk, Nik. I'm sorry. Do you think you can put up with me?"

Nikki grinned at him. "I'll have to think about that."

"Things between us will have to change, you know," he began. "I mean, when we get really close, I don't like what happens to me. Well, actually, I *do* like it. All that kissing and stuff. I just can't seem to quit—I mean, I just—" He stopped, looking uncomfortable. "Maybe that's why we shouldn't spend so much time alone together."

"I know. You're right, Jeff. It'll be a lot better if we spend more time with other people. Not just for us, but for them, too. We can't keep cutting off all our friends like we've been doing. I want to go back and be the best friend I can to Keesha, and Hollis, too. And even to Noel, if she'll let me. I think she's really going to need a friend. And I'll visit Chad, or write to him if they won't let me visit." She stopped for a breath and Jeff smiled at her.

"Anything else?" he asked, grinning.

"Yeah, there is," Nikki said. "I made up my mind a month ago to spend time with God every day—really spend time, not just go through the motions. But I haven't done it. I keep saying I'm too busy, but if I found time to spend at least an hour every day on the phone with you, I'm not really too busy." She looked at him apologetically. "I'm afraid I won't be able to talk to you nearly as much, Jeff."

He nodded. "That's one of the things I was thinking, too. If I say my whole life belongs to God, that includes my time, doesn't it? All I've been thinking about is getting to the phone to talk with you."

Nikki swallowed hard. "I'm gonna miss those phone calls, but you're right. I didn't want to admit it at first, but you are. And no matter what we have to give up for now, I want to do this right, Jeff Allen. I may have gotten it all wrong the first time, but God's letting me start over. In His eyes, I'm as clean now as if I never messed up, and I'm going to keep it that way."

❧ *Epilogue* ❧

DEAR JEFF,

Okay, so you were right about this, too. Maybe this "talking" by e-mail isn't quite as good as talking on the phone, but it does help me feel like we're in touch without spending hours at it. I even have time during the week to get my homework done, imagine that! But I have to confess, I sure do look forward to the weekends when we really do talk.

Mom's ankle is a lot better. She said on the phone that she's getting pretty good at using crutches. The thing she's really upset about is that the doctor told her to get rid of all her high heels!

Seriously, though, something pretty incredible happened yesterday. She called me and said my dad was in church. He didn't stay after to talk or anything, and he still won't return her phone calls, but he was there. I'd like it better if all my prayers got answered immediately, you know? But I'm going to keep praying about this one. I don't know what will happen, but I know God will do what's right.

You know how I told you Hollis has been eating lunch with Keesha and me a lot? Well, Hollis has so many questions, I suggested we start meeting before school on Wednesday mornings for a Bible study. We went and asked Mr. Peabody about it during study hall. At first he said it probably wasn't legal, but then he finally decided we could. Keesha's got some friends she says will come, and Hollis thinks that Noel may come someday, too.

I got a letter from Chad today. They won't let anybody see him right now except his family, but he wants to know if I could write him. Regularly, I mean. He's getting help there—there's all kinds of counselors, I guess—not just for the depression but for the drinking, too. But I think he needs more than just that. So I was wondering, Jeff, how would you feel about both you and me writing him? He told me once I was the only one he could talk to, but I think he needs a guy to talk to, too. Think about it, okay?

Mom says T.J. is at the college group at her church all the time, now. She's pretty excited how all this is turning out.

Okay, we agreed to take no more than 10 minutes writing each night and my time's up. So I'm signing off, for now.

Love,
Nikki